AF592833

Paws Around the World

Paws Around the World

Prachi Sharma

NU VOICE
PRESS

First published by NU VOICE PRESS 2025
An imprint of Hubhawks Pvt. Ltd
www.nuvoicepress.com

Copyright © Prachi Sharma 2025

The moral rights of the author have been asserted
Database right Nu Voice Press (maker)

This is a work of fiction. Space and time have been rearranged to suit the convenience of the book. Except for public figures, hotels, and institution names, any resemblance to persons living or dead or the real events are purely coincidental. The opinions expressed in the book are those of the characters, and should not be confused with that of the Author.

All rights reserved. Enquiries concerning reproduction outside the scope of the above should be sent to Nu Voice Press at the address above.

ISBN: 978-81-994254-5-3
Typeset by Pooja Sharma
Printed at Manipal Technologies Limited, Manipal
Published by Nu Voice Press

Hold your horses tight, as my story is going to get wild. A few of you will reach the finish line, a few of you will leave in between, but each one of you will have a ride to remember!

—Oreo the Dog.

Chapter 1

On a stormy night in June 2007, or so I've been told, amid lightning flashes and thundering skies, I was born with my seven siblings in a small, abandoned shed. I'm not sure of my name or family lineage, but does it even matter? If it does, then it's my mother's human family you should get hold of, who didn't even record my birth details!

I am a mix of Labrador and Doberman, inheriting the best traits of both the breeds. People often comment about how lucky I am to have the cuteness of a Labrador and the sturdiness of a Doberman. My humans definitely hit the jackpot with me! They sure do get a lot of attention when people notice my unique mix.

The morning after my birth, I was woken up by a sudden and intense burst of activity. I opened my eyes and saw the vast clear sky first. Loud noises diverted my attention, and I saw that there was a huge van standing next to my home. People were coming out of it. They were dressed in white coats and were shouting. There was chaos everywhere, and some of them moved closer to my shed. I felt a pang of panic going down my spine. I didn't know what was happening, but it sure didn't seem pleasing. I looked around. My brothers and sisters were equally scared too.

Before long, the van filled with hundreds of other dogs stopped right in front of the shed. Before I could look at my mother for support, my mother, siblings, and I were picked up unceremoniously and thrown into it by two skinny guys. The space inside the van was so tight that we ended up piled on top of each other. I was pushed to one corner. There was a big dog who was barking a lot, and it was scaring me. I tried looking for my pack. That is when my mother jumped in front of me and snarled the bully away. I was exhausted, and slept next to my brother.

The sudden jerk woke me from my nap. The van stopped with a sharp brake. The strong smell of dog pee reached us even before we were out of the van. The four men began their work as soon as we were taken out of the vehicle. We were all taken inside a small house. They moved us, one-day-old pups, to a room separate from our mothers. I was famished; the smell from the other room made my mouth water. Oh, the aroma of the food! I began to cry. Soon, my siblings joined in, and it was a very noisy affair. Each crunch of mommy's bite made me hungrier. Thankfully, after she was done eating, she came to our room. My siblings and I were elated to see her. I rushed to hug her legs. Then I had milk, and after an exhausting morning, went to sleep.

We have been here for almost a week. I was used to the routine by now. In the morning, the incredible nurse, who was caring for me with affection and dedication, would gently cradle me in her arms and take me for a walk outside the nursery. Once in the garden, she would put me down on the soft ground, and I would get busy scrounging for food and sniffing all the wonderful smells around me. Looking at me brought her joy, and why would it not? I was a golden-brown puppy with hair softer than silk. And my eyes, they were my best feature; I had big eyes and a chiselled face with a sharp chin. Yes, I was handsome even at that tender age. We would spend around an hour or so this way before she brought me back to the comfort of my nursery and fed me. The same routine followed in the evenings as well.

One day, when she cradled me in her arms like she usually did and I drifted off, anticipating our planned walk, she handed me to a man who stroked my back gently. Let me tell you a secret right now—I preferred humans over my species! Being petted was the most enjoyable thing in the world for me, so I found myself in a state of pure bliss when the man scratched my ears and neck.

I settled into the man's arms, thinking he'd be taking me for my daily walk, but to my utter surprise, he began walking towards a car. Soon, I was placed on the passenger seat. I was filled with a whirlwind of emotions and confusion. The man sat in the driver's seat next to me and drove us away from my sanctuary. Questions raced through my mind: Why was I being moved away from my mother and brothers? Had I done something wrong?

The pain of separation was overwhelming. I felt as if I was abandoned. All I wanted was to reunite with my family—my siblings and my mother. My non-stop howling and crying did not make him stop or turn the car around. Humans had sealed my fate, without even asking me once. They moved me away from my family.

Here I was, being moved again, even though I had barely been alive for ten days.

Confused and scared, I closed my eyes in resignation. Nothing was in my paws, so I surrendered to my fate. After what seemed like an eternity, the car stopped. The man scooped me up and said, "Welcome home, Oreo. Don't worry, we will love you and take good care of you."

I was confused. *Who is Oreo?*

"Honey, come out. Oreo is here."

A woman came running out of the house carrying a spatula in one of her hands. Her hair was long, flowing gently and swaying in the wind, framing a face adorned with a warm, genuine smile. Her eyes sparkled with kindness, and her demeanour radiated a friendly warmth that drew me towards her. She took me in her arms and started dancing joyfully. She halted briefly, kissed me on my muzzle and said, "Oreo, you are adorable. I love you."

This was when I realised, *I* was Oreo. *But when did they name me? No one even bothered to ask me.* I started to seethe with anger, but then it dawned on me that no one had asked me before separating me from my family too. So, I accepted that my opinion did not matter to anyone in this world.

The kisses on my face snapped me back to reality. I looked at the joy in the lady's eyes and sighed. It was not that bad at all. I was in a good place. The house had two rooms and a balcony, which was the best part. It was inside a big building with big walls and a huge gate. The tree next to the balcony chirped with birds. I had my own place to sleep. They did not tie me, and I was able to roam around the house. Both my humans loved me. To be honest, I was adorable, so credit goes to me. But yes, it could have been worse.

I did my best to adapt. The first three months of my life with them were full of ups and downs. My new humans were doing the best they could; I tell ya, they did. On the first day itself, they gave me a cosy bed, a bowl of fresh water and milk. I devoured the milk and slept off the rest of the day, feeling exhausted after the long road trip.

I felt content until the next morning. After refilling my bowl of milk and water, both my humans shut the door behind them, started their cars and left.

I was shocked to say the least. How could my humans abandon me? Confused and alone, I howled and paced. Fear consumed me. What if this place caught fire? What if robbers or murderers came? What if my humans never returned? My anxiety wouldn't let me eat or drink. I tried to lick milk a couple of times because it was my favourite thing in the world, but it wouldn't go down my throat. So, I kept on crying the whole day.

Only when I heard the car in the evening did I relax. *Oh, boy... What a relief!*

"Oreo, you didn't drink your milk. What happened, my baby?" My human mother asked as soon as she opened the door, concern evident on her face.

In that moment, I forgot everything and leapt up with joy, wagging my tail and licking their faces. When she offered me milk, I quickly gulped it down. Content with happiness and feeling safe in the knowledge that my humans will not leave me alone ever again, I forgave them for this mistake and drifted off to sleep.

The next morning, I woke up thinking I would be around my humans. But to my utter shock, they left again. This became a pattern. They left at 9:00 a.m. and returned at 7:00 p.m. every day. Those eight to nine hours were pure torture for me. I couldn't eat or relax, overwhelmed with loneliness. I was missing my pack and my mother a lot. When I was with them, we were always together, be it on the street or shelter. As the days passed, I kept on losing weight when I should have been growing.

One Sunday morning, I was lying on my bed. The day was cloudy, and I felt equally dull. There was no energy to chase the birds or even eat. My humans looked at me, immediately lifted me in their arms, and made me sit in the car. As the car started, I braced for another long ride, but to my surprise, it turned out to be a short one. In about fifteen minutes, we stopped in front of a hospital. The scent of that place reminded me of the day I was born. Remembering the overwhelming commotion that followed my birth, I felt repulsed by the hospital.

I feared my humans would abandon me again and braced myself for separation. As they pulled on my leash, I tried to hold off by standing my ground, but I had little strength. I was just a month old, and starved on top of that. Before long, I was pulled into a cabin. A man stood there, looming over me in his white coat. His eyes seemed to pop out of his glasses! He was smiling while looking at me, but I didn't like that smile even for a second! And my instincts were right, as this man conducted a thorough examination, probing every part of my body. He gave me big injections as well. I felt extremely drowsy after that and barely remembered the ride back home.

Over the next two months, we visited the vet twice more for follow-ups and more injections.

"Oreo, you need to eat. You can't survive without eating. Injections can't keep you alive," my human mother said, tears in her eyes.

I felt very bad for making my mother cry. I tried to eat and be a good and obedient dog, but I could not. I did not know how to be happy in the long hours of their absence.

With their jobs and busy lives, they realised they couldn't care for me properly.

Chapter 2

I was sleeping on the balcony of the house. My humans were inside, and it was a beautiful day with a caressing light breeze. I had just had food, and I was feeling content and happy. I saw a car stop in front of the house and three people came out. One of them started moving towards my house. As a loyal protector, I started barking. A young adult man wearing specs came to our door despite my warning. He was surely brave.

The other boy and the girl accompanying him kept their distance from me. They would steal glances in my direction, their eyes filled with fear, uncertainty, and confusion—emotions that mirrored my own.

My family came out and gave me the shock of my life.

"Oreo, we are not able to take care of you properly. We have found this new family for you. They will love you and care for you. We will always love you," my humans said regretfully.

I was not able to believe what had just happened. Suddenly, the day became the worst, and my happiness was engulfed by fear.

With a final kiss from my previous family, I was handed over to this new family. The man at the door took me in his arms; he smelled like lemons. He was warm in his touch as he patted my head and held me in his arms, whispering words of comfort. He tried his best to make me feel safe. If only it were that simple.

He carried me to his car, and I saw my old family. They were standing behind, crying. I wanted to stay with them. I didn't want to go away from my human mother too. But no one asked me. I didn't have a choice. But do we ever? All we can do is go with the flow... and I did. I glanced back, hoping to see my family running after me, eager to stop me from going, but there was no one. I realised that day that such miracles are rare. I decided to embrace my fate once again.

I tried to find comfort in the fact that I was moving to a new home and not being abandoned on the street or hit by a car. My family had found me a new home, for better or worse. Neither they knew how it would turn out, nor did I. Well, I am going off topic here. I apologise. Reflecting on the past can have this effect on one. Who am I but a little dog who sometimes loves to reminisce? We all secretly love to, don't we?

Coming back to the story; I wagged my tail hoping to charm my new family members, aiming to reduce their sense of unease. Despite my own fears, I attempted to show maturity. The girl, who was similar in age to the man carrying me, refused to meet my gaze. If only she had looked at me, I swear she would not have been able to resist the charm of puppy eyes. She sat in one corner of the back seat, and I stayed in the opposite corner, not wanting to make a bad impression on my first day. At three months old, I had already changed homes twice. I think I was born with rollers on my paws.

After forty-five minutes of travel, mostly spent stuck in Bangalore's notorious traffic, we arrived at a single-family home. It was a double-storey house with large windows overlooking the gate and a balcony on the upper floor. A staircase on the side of the house caught my eye–I ought to explore it later. As we entered the main gate, I saw an elderly woman peeking from the front window with amusement. When we went inside, I wanted to roam around and explore the house, but fear held me back. I sat by the door and whimpered quietly as I looked around feeling anxious. I sat beside the good human who had driven me here. He introduced himself as Nikhil. He then went on to introduce me to the rest of the family.

"Here, Oreo, this is Mummy," Nikhil said, pointing to the woman whom I saw in the window. Her eyes exuded warmth. She was tall, and her personality commanded respect. No idea why, but I bowed down a little.

"You've already met Lipika and Manish. They are siblings. Welcome home, boy."

"What do you mean Manish is my brother? Is he not yours as well?" Lipika asked furiously.

"Of course, he is... but he is more than that for me. After all, he is the only brother of my wife," Nikhil said, trying to pacify Lipika.

If looking and turning away counts as a meeting, then I met them. Lipika and Manish awkwardly stood in the living room. They maintained their distance from me as if I were untouchable.

"Oreo, Papa is not here right now. He has gone away for work. He will be back after two weeks. But don't worry, you will get to meet the rest of the family soon," Lipika explained.

Suddenly, Nikhil jumped from his chair. "Oh, how could I forget about his bed?" He muttered to himself.

Then there was a commotion.

"Where will he sleep?" Lipika asked.

"We need to set up a comfortable place for him to sleep," Nikhil said.

There was significant activity in the house afterwards. Manish rummaged for a mat, likely intending to create a comfortable spot for me. But then Nikhil took charge, carefully placing me on the mat. However, with my twisting and turning, it was clear that the mat was not comfortable.

Recognising this, they quickly decided to find something more suitable. Soon after, they returned with a small basket lined with soft towels for warmth. Despite their efforts, it was clear that my new bed was too small for me.

As preparations continued, Mummy called from the kitchen, directing attention to what would become my bed—a large, orange-coloured basket. It was a bit damp and carried the faint aroma of spices, but Lipika carefully cleaned and dried it off. Following this, Manish layered it with sheets, bed covers, and some old towels, transforming it into a cosy and comfortable place for me to rest. They positioned it beside the door, creating a designated spot for me.

Mummy, ever vigilant, then handed over a green-coloured blanket to Nikhil, ensuring I had extra warmth when it got chilly in the middle of the night. To confine me, they tied a rope loosely around my neck and secured it to the window in the living room, establishing a perimeter to keep me safe.

The setting in the house was meticulously arranged for both functionality and comfort. In the enormous hall, alongside my designated spot, there was a bed and a wooden sofa. A staircase stood adjacent to the front wall, leading to different levels of the house. The hall had two distinct sides—one leading to the kitchen, bustling with activity, and the other leading to a narrow hallway. This hallway hosted two doors—one leading to a bathroom and the other opening into a room, offering glimpses into the various spaces that made up the warm and welcoming home. There was a big portrait on the wall of the living room. Some people seemed familiar, and I was keenly observing the portrait.

"What will he eat?" Lipika's voice interrupted my thoughts. She talked a lot. Ever since I entered the house, all I remember is hearing her loud, piercing voice. "Shall we try milk?"

Mummy handed Nikhil a bowl of milk. I tried to drink, but although I was hungry, I couldn't. The experience of shifting from my old house, bidding farewell to my old humans, and meeting my new family was overwhelming. I was missing them. I remembered I saw a portrait where people seemed familiar, maybe my family was there. Maybe they are here too. I went again to the portrait and started searching for my family there.

"Oreo, this is your new family." Lipika said, smashing all my hopes.

"You have already met Nikhil, me, Manish and Mummy. That young girl you see with specs, that is Chhoti. She is studying in Hyderabad. She is the youngest, and you will love her. She is just full of energy. And that girl you see with long hair, she is Prabalika. She is younger than me and is working in Mumbai. She is also planning to come and meet you with her husband when she gets time off. That guy with broad shoulders and specs, yes, that one," she said, pointing her finger to a fair young man with specs. "He is Brijmohan. He can be your personal on-call doctor. That would be nice, right? And that is Papa," she said as she gestured towards a man in his fifties. What I noticed first was his kind eyes. He had the same innocence and maturity I saw on Mummy's face.

Okay, not the family where I came from. I sighed and resigned to my bed.

I drifted off to sleep, as Nikhil sat beside me and petted me the entire time. I heard the chatter dying down as the family went to bed after dinner.

Manish slept in the hall on the *settee*; Mummy went to the downstairs bedroom, and Lipika and Nikhil proceeded upstairs. After a few minutes, there was an eerie silence in the house. The lights were out, and other than the humming of the fridge, the house was silent. They had placed my bed in the foyer, next to the front door, right beside the shoe rack—away from the rest of the house. I was also not used to being away from my humans during the night. Silence beckoned loneliness, and that is when the reality of my situation came crashing down upon me—I no longer had my dog or human family with me. I had a panic attack. I started whimpering, which slowly turned to moaning and then howling. I felt a heaviness in my heart. Fear and homesickness overwhelmed me.

The hall lights switched on, and Manish came running. "What happened? Are you okay? Do you need something?"

Well, *duh*! I need cuddling and love. I'm frozen with terror.

"Wait a minute. Let me call Nikhil *jijaji*," he said.

Within two minutes, the whole family gathered in the hall. Nikhil scooped me up in his arms and petted me.

I was still scared of what was happening to me and being away from my family. No matter how much they petted me, my howling did not stop.

A constant knock on the door diverted the attention though.

"Who could it be at this hour?" Manish said, opening the door.

"Do you know what time it is? Don't you know this is a residential area?" A bald, well-built man was shouting.

"Sorry about that..." Manish began.

"What sorry, *haan*? You're disturbing everyone's sleep." He was not ready to listen.

"Mr Arora, just listen to me once..." Manish tried again.

"You guys are not fit to be here!"

"Mr Arora, this is a three-month-old puppy who came here just this evening. He's already moved houses twice at this tender age, and it was he who was crying." Nikhil said, taking me to the door in his arms.

"Yes, just give him a few nights, and he will get adjusted. He might even help us all by chasing the squirrels and cats away," Manish added, laughing.

Mr Arora looked at me and calmed down a little.

"Oh, it's a puppy... I was thinking some loud music is playing," he said awkwardly.

"*Arey*, Arora *beta*, I am here. How can you think there will be loud music at this hour with me in the house?" Mummy asked.

"Sorry, Aunty. Good night." He said and finally left.

Their kindness overwhelmed me, and I realised they will always have my back.

When I joined this family, I was sick, mostly because of malnutrition. My previous family was seldom home, and I never enjoyed eating alone. I only knew how to drink water and milk—nothing else. Ironically, despite being a dog, food wasn't my priority. Faced with the shocks of shifting homes and families, my mind was preoccupied with existential concerns. Fear of the unknown, feelings of abandonment, and despair often engulfed me. These emotions consumed my thoughts and energy, making it challenging to focus on everyday priorities like eating properly. As a result, I was unintentionally neglecting my dietary needs, leading to weight loss and declining health. I ended up being sick.

Once the rest of the family other than Nikhil overcame their initial shock at having an animal in the house, they embraced me. Yes, it was only Nikhil who wanted me in the house. Rest all were not ready.

"He needs to eat."

"We should consult the vet."

"There's a veterinary clinic on the next street. Let's take him there."

And so, I was taken to the vet. The clinic was small, more like a house. The vet acted like the ward boy, nurse, and pharmacist. He examined me.

"He is underweight. How often does he eat?" the doctor asked.

"He doesn't eat. We leave dog food out all day, but he doesn't touch it," answered Nikhil.

"He drinks one cup of milk in the morning," Lipika added.

"He needs to eat. Try curd, baby food, and pureed vegetables. Bring him back in twenty days. If he hasn't improved, we might have to inject glucose." The doctor looked worried. "We will give him his rabies vaccine now. Let me check his vitals before that."

The doctor got a big syringe and a cotton swab. Nikhil picked me up and placed me on the examination table. The doctor pressed my chest and lungs, then he poked a long tube inside my buttocks.

"The temperature is also fine; we can give him the vaccine," he concluded, taking out that tube.

Saying this, the doctor started massaging my left hind leg. I was quite enjoying that, when a sharp prick jerked me.

"All done, Oreo," Nikhil said. He was constantly petting me and holding me during the whole process.

I didn't even yelp; I am such a brave boy. Even the doctor commented, "Good boy, Oreo. You're quite sweet." To Nikhil he said, "You're really lucky that he is so friendly."

To anyone who fears needles, I will say this: they don't hurt—they're over-hyped. It's just a prick, like an ant sting. Though I wouldn't choose to get one! No one likes ant stings either. Anyway, after the injection, I was left to roam around the cabin while Nikhil and Lipika spoke to the doctor. They might have been talking about me, but I only cared about marking my territory. It was an ideal place, given the number of female dogs that visit. I had to secure my domain. The challenging part was finding the hidden spots to mark, not the small injection prick. Did I mention how strong and level-headed I am?

"Oreo!"

Mid-pee on the sofa in the exam room, I heard Nikhil shout. I still don't understand his issue. No one stopped him if he wanted to mark the territory. And he should understand—we're family. After all, what I mark is his too. These people, I tell ya.

"Sorry, Doctor."

"It's okay. I am used to it."

"So, we'll have to force-feed him," Lipika said, continuing the conversation.

The doctor nodded.

After paying the doctor his fee, we all made our way outside and Manish said, "You guys go home, I will get Cerelac."

"He might eat once he works up an appetite. I'll take him for a long walk in the meantime. Let's meet here in half an hour." Nikhil said, bidding goodbye to Manish and Lipika.

I went with Nikhil, wagging my tail, looking forward to the bonus walk.

So, this is how my whole family accompanied me to my first important vet visit with them. Although it looked like we were all going to an annual fair, I appreciated everyone's support and enthusiasm.

It was dark by the time we returned home, and I entered the house with Manish and Lipika carrying five different flavours of Cerelac. Lipika arranged all the packets by my bed, while Mummy brought out a bowl of milk and another of curd at Nikhil's request. Wasting no time, they all got to work.

They opened the first packet and mixed a spoonful of Cerelac with milk. They tried to feed it to me. I cringed my nose and moved my face away from the citrus paste.

"He doesn't like orange flavour," Manish said.

Lipika added, "Let's try wheat and apple."

They opened another packet and mixed a spoonful. I sniffed it. It was mild. I licked the spoon—sweet! I licked more.

"He likes it!" Exclaimed Nikhil.

"Mummy, he likes apples," Manish shouted.

"Let's try the third one too, vegetable and rice, and see if he likes it better."

The next spoonful tasted like chalk—it was tasteless and odourless. I spit it out.

"Well, he doesn't seem to like this one either. So, apple it is," Lipika commented.

Manish quickly added, "Let's feed him apple Cerelac before he starts crying."

They mixed apple and wheat flavour Cerelac with yogurt and fed me spoon after spoon. I managed to eat six-seven spoons before feeling full. I still wasn't used to eating semi-solid food.

"This is not enough. You're a big boy, Oreo." Lipika looked around at Manish, Nikhil and Mummy and added, "We need to feed him more. We'll have to *force-feed* him."

I was curious about 'force-feed.' Lipika kept mentioning it again and again. Maybe it meant a new dish? Well, it wasn't long before I learned what the word meant. What a nightmare, I tell ya!

When everyone agreed to force-feed me, Lipika emerged from the kitchen with a bowl and a plastic object that looked like a spoon. She filled it with some thick orange liquid, held my mouth, and pushed the syringe in. The disgusting liquid filled my mouth. I tried to spit it out, but she closed my mouth and lifted my neck. I had no choice but to swallow.

"What is this?" Asked Nikhil, holding me down.

"Boiled carrot and apple puree," Lipika said.

"He doesn't seem to like it."

"He has no choice but to eat with the syringe. Right, Oreo?" she said, smiling and looking at me. *Why don't you try it then?* I thought, but kept quiet. You see, I am well-mannered too.

As much as I would hate to agree with her, she was right. The vet had given strict orders: I needed to be fed, be it with a syringe or spoon. Otherwise, I would end up in the hospital because of extreme dehydration and fatigue.

This cycle repeated countless times until the bowl was empty. If they wanted to get rid of that muck, why not throw it down the drain or the trash can? Why feed it to me?

I lay in bed, recuperating. To my horror, Lipika returned a couple of hours later, now with curd and Cerelac. And this continued for the next fifteen days. Sometimes it was carrot puree, apple and carrot puree, peas and spinach puree, curd and Cerelac, or glucose water. It seemed like she enjoyed torturing me. I started hating the sight of her and the syringe. I tried to retreat and hide, but she always caught me. I think she is a secret agent! Once, they forgot to put on my leash. So, when I heard her steps, I quickly jumped out and went under the sofa. I knew she wouldn't be able to ever find me. I saw her steps reaching my basket. She called out my name. She asked others if they had seen me. No one had. It was so funny! I had outdone them. As I was sitting and smiling away in glory, I felt a hand slip inside and pull me out. Lipika was standing with me in one hand and a syringe in another!

As much as I hated it, I would have to confess that by the seventh day, I was starting to feel very energetic. I could go for longer walks and play for hours without getting tired. Even the flavour of carrot and apple puree became less unpleasant. I began to feel a new sensation in my stomach—hunger. I finally felt compelled to eat. When Lipika fed me some milk-soaked bread, I instantly fell in love with food. It was love at first bite!

"Let's make another visit to the doctor," Lipika suggested, indicating a follow-up appointment.

Everyone agreed and within the next half an hour, we were at the doctor's clinic. "Again, the same gang. This family visits the vet office as if it's a fair!"

I felt nervous not knowing what treatment he would suggest this time. But I felt much better than the last time I had visited the clinic because my belly was full.

"He looks good. He has gained weight too," the doctor observed, expressing satisfaction with my progress. He checked me all over. "Continue whatever it is you are doing as it seems to be working," he advised. "But you can stop feeding him with a syringe and get him used to eating normally."

This brought big smiles of relief on my family's faces. And of course, mine too.

"I won't be giving him any medicine, but he needs deworming injections," the doctor recommended.

After three injections, we returned home.

At home, Lipika repeated everything the doctor had said to Mummy, including that I could now be fed normally without a syringe.

"Cerelac mixed with curd and bread dipped in milk. We will start with these two," Lipika suggested, outlining the menu for me.

As the journey continued, the discussion on my menu continued. Everyone seemed involved in planning what would be best for me.

"Now, he needs to eat by himself. No more spoon-feeding," Nikhil instructed Lipika and Manish, indicating a shift in feeding approach.

That evening, when the bowl of milk-soaked bread was kept beside my bed, there was no syringe. I waited for them to come and feed me, but no one did. As much as I disliked the process of being force-fed, I enjoyed being fed by my family. I *wanted* them to come and feed me. I kept on waiting; if they were resolute, so was I. I returned to my bed without touching the food.

As I sat quietly on my bed, I kept on looking at the bowl which had my favourite food, and Nikhil, who sat on the bed in the living room, watching TV with the others.

Lipika whispered something to Nikhil, and he loudly replied, “Let him be hungry, he will learn to eat on his own.”

After a while when Mummy started to lose her resolve and got up to check on me, Nikhil told her, “No, Mummy. Oreo needs to learn to eat on his own. He will eat whenever he gets too hungry. No more spoon-feeding.”

“Okay,” and “Fine,” they replied.

By then, I was hungry, but I refused to surrender. I wanted to be spoon-fed and was ready to test everyone's limits. When I resigned myself to going without dinner, I noticed Nikhil walking towards me with a spoon. He drew the curtains in the living room and started feeding me, spoon by spoon.

As Nikhil fed me, I glimpsed two amused faces peeking at us—Manish and Lipika.

“Manish, wasn't there a *strict* no-spoon-feeding rule?” Lipika asked rhetorically, smirking at Nikhil.

“I think it only applies to us,” Manish replied.

“He is still weak and needs to be fed however he likes,” Nikhil replied.

This marked my first triumph in the house, my first training lesson for the family. They would have to spoon-feed me for the rest of their lives. I resolved. Lesson 1: done successfully.

But training was not fully complete. They did try to make me eat on my own. They tried, honest to God, they did. They left the food for me and went away. I would refuse to eat. They waited for forty minutes, then picked it up and did not give me anything for the rest of the night. I was fine with it. You need to be strong when you are training someone. They would again bring my food to me in the morning and leave it for me to eat. I abstained from eating. They were working on training me, and I was working on training them. Guess who won?

Chapter 3

"Manish, have you looked at his eyes?" Lipika asked. She was sitting near me.

"Why are they red? Do we need to take him to the doctor? Shall I call a cab?" Manish came running.

"No, they are cute."

"See, he has such innocent eyes."

Suddenly I found two pairs of eyes staring into mine. These two can be really dramatic. I sighed and put my head down.

"Wow! Oreo, you have the world's best eyes. I love you!" Lipika exclaimed.

"Yeah, that is true. Looking into his eyes makes you want to protect him and be with him," Manish added.

Now my bed was shifted to the inside of the house. The orange basket was now near the window facing the door, beside the staircase to the upper floor. I tried to act calm, stretching my legs and resuming sleeping, but my heart was dancing. I was in!

I looked at her, amused at how expressive she was. *Someone needs to grow up*. I then made a slow regal walk to my basket. I knew they were looking at me.

I don't want to brag, but I was a sight to behold.

A few more days passed, and I settled into a routine. Nikhil walked me in the mornings and evenings, and I slept the rest of the day. With Mummy at home, I never felt lonely.

Whenever she cooked in the kitchen, I would go and sit next to the kitchen door. And she would talk to me.

"Oreo, *daal khaoge*?" She would ask.

"Oreo, do you know today is Vasant Panchmi? It's the celebration of spring." She taught me a lot about culture as well.

"Oreo, do you miss your mother?" She would ask me sometimes.

Thoughts of my mother would make me whimper, and then she would shower pearls of wisdom on me.

"*Beta,* always live life in the present. I know we form connections and relations, and we are social beings. But, in a nutshell, life is all about the present. You have spent some time with your mom, cherish that. But do not let that stop you from growing."

When she watched TV in the evenings, I would sit by her sofa.

"Oreo, you are also into *Anupama* now. Let's see what hurdle she crosses today," she would joke.

A gentle and caring soul, she would make me feel loved and protected.

But she did not pet me a lot. Whenever I stood by her bed, she'd lovingly pet my forehead and say, "This is it, Oreo. This is all I can do." I felt content with that.

Lipika, on the other hand, would pet me even during my walks!

Though my species likes being pampered, even we have limits. *Give me some space, lady!* I thought. Her curly hair bothered me a lot too. Whenever she bent to kiss me or hug me (which, believe me, was more than a hundred times a day), her hair would prick me. And don't let me get started on the shrillness of her voice. It was like thousands of decibels rolled in one. I'd let her pet me once, then move away.

Once I had trained my family to spoon-feed me, I wanted to be able to sleep with them. Hence followed the second training lesson for them.

I never liked sleeping in that orange basket. On nights when the clouds thundered and rain splashed across the windows, I felt like someone was out there to get me. The trees were banging fiercely against the walls. The howling wind didn't make anything better. I curled in my bed for safety. My family was sleeping soundly without any care. When lightning cracked through the sky, bringing trees down with it, I peed in my bed. I was no longer able to handle the cruel dance of nature.

That is when I decided to take matters into my own paws.

I got out of bed, stood next to the stairs, and started whimpering. The rain drowned out my feeble sounds, failing to wake Manish sleeping in the hall. I tried louder but to no avail. The rain was hitting the windowpanes hard, and I feared it might break. My bed was just beside the window, so I ran from there and curled up near the shoe stand which was next to the main door. But the sound of the lightning screeching through the door made me run from there too. I went to the kitchen and realised the sounds were not that deafening here. I walked further inside and settled behind a big tin in the pantry. It was cosy; finally, I was able to breathe.

"Oreo? Oreo, good morning!" Lipika shrieked as she came down the stairs. "Manish, have you seen him?"

"Oreo? No, I just woke up. He must be near the front door ready for his walk."

"He is not here as well," Lipika said from the door.

"Give him a few minutes, he will come out on his own."

"Where is Oreo? *Aaj aaya nahin*?" Mummy asked, coming out of her room a little later.

"Now even I am worried," Manish said.

Nikhil, Lipika, and Manish started searching in every room.

"Oreo... Oreo!" I was hearing all the commotion, but was I ready to let them know I am safe?

No, not yet. None of them listened to my whimpers last night, now they can worry a little.

"Did he go out?" Nikhil asked.

"But how? Doors are still locked," Manish replied.

"I checked under the beds in all the rooms as well."

"He is not even on the balcony," Manish shouted.

"Mummy, where could he be?" Lipika's worries grew.

"*Ghar mein hi hoga. Chinta mat karo,*" Mummy reassured. "Oreo, *beta?*"

Now when she called, I had to come out. Slowly, I crawled out of my safe spot behind the wheat flour tin and stood next to her.

"There you are!" All of them chimed together. Nikhil picked me up his arms and hugged me tight.

"You scared us, Oreo!"

"Why were you hiding there?" Manish asked.

"Oh, because of yesterday's storm. Oh, poor you!" Now they realised.

"You could have crawled into my bed, Oreo," Manish said.

From then on, I slept in Manish's bed too. The following night, even without rain, I climbed into bed with him.

"Come, Oreo, you can sleep with me tonight," Manish reaffirmed as I jumped onto his bed.

With Manish's hand over me, I had the best sleep in ages. From then on, I'd pick one of them each night to ensure no one felt left out. I believe in equality, so I occasionally did night shifts—half the night on Manish's bed, then sneaking upstairs to sleep beside Lipika, snuggled at her feet.

"You both will spoil him," Nikhil kept saying.

"Exactly. Why do you have to make him sleep on your bed?" Mummy added. "He has his own bed and sleeps there during the day. He can sleep there at night too."

"But he feels lonely, Mummy, and he is a little baby. Look at him, how innocent," Manish and Lipika said.

The two people who initially refused to even acknowledge my presence were now arguing on my behalf. That's my charm!

"We'll get him a trainer, don't worry," Lipika and Manish said.

Chapter 4

I heard a doorbell, and as usual, ran towards the door.

"Wait, Oreo."

Positioned behind Lipika, I was prepared to jump and lick anyone entering. I'm always a delightful host, ready with kisses and appreciation.

The door swung open, revealing a man around five feet tall with a noticeably protruding belly. Something about his demeanour made me retreat. I didn't even lick him.

"Hi, I'm Ramesh, the dog trainer. Manish gave me this address."

"Hi, Ramesh. I'm Lipika. Please come in." As they were making their way into the living room, Lipika introduced me to the angry-looking man, "By the way, this is Oreo. Your new student."

The man greeted me with a broad smile. "Hi, puppy."

Puppy? Who calls a *dog* a puppy? I disliked him immediately.

"What kind of training do you give to dogs?" Lipika began her interrogation, and I returned to my bed, showing how well-behaved I was.

"Who is it, Lipika?" Mummy asked, coming out of her room.

"Mummy, it's the trainer."

Then the man answered Lipika's question, "I train dogs from three months to three years old. I use a stick and this clicker for training."

"You use the stick to hit them?" She asked, shocked.

"No, no, just to scare them with the sound."

"Do you have any treats?" When Lipika and Mummy shook their heads, he added, "You will need to buy some for training."

"Okay, we'll get them. Will you start training today or tomorrow?"

"Let's begin today itself. I will take him for a walk, and start by training him to walk beside you, or anyone who is handling him on the road."

"Great, sounds good!" Lipika exclaimed excitedly. She turned to me and said, "Oreo, you ready? Time to go for a walk."

Although I had reservations about the new man, it was, after all, a matter of an evening walk, so I could not refuse. In any case, I didn't think I had any choice in the matter. Before long, I left with the man; he hadn't done me any harm yet, but I felt uneasy. Lipika followed us to the front gate. He held the leash at a distance, not pulling it much, so I relaxed. We walked in comfortable silence until we turned, and I saw a cat. I sprinted towards it, and that's when I felt the stick on my legs.

"Stop," he shouted. I stopped because of the pain in my knee.

He yanked the leash and pulled me towards him.

"Walk," instructed the man, and we started walking again.

He yanked my leash every time I tried to sniff the garbage or move faster. The yanking hurt my neck, but the worst was yet to come.

We reached the parking lot of the office building on the opposite street. He paused, lit a cigarette and started smoking. Didn't he know smoking is injurious to health and passive smoking harms, too? I tried to move away from him as I loved my life and my lungs!

"Sit," he barked, hitting my leg with the stick.

Who was he to tell me to sit? I did not sit.

"Sit," he growled again. Unsure, I wagged my tail in response. I thought it was better to be friends, especially after seeing his 'wild' side. Trust me, I did give him enough signals.

But right at that moment, he used the clicker. A sharp sensation shot through my body, transfixing me on the spot. I didn't know what to do, as if my mind was fogged. I felt like I was dying. I doubted I'd ever see my family again—the family who grew to love me, whom I loved more than anything else.

After an hour of standing there while he smoked and talked to other dog walkers, we finally walked back towards the house. I was beyond relieved.

Upon entering the front door, I ran to Mummy's room. She was taking a nap. I just sat there, looking at her, thanking my stars for how kind she was as a human being. I instantly felt better... safer.

"How was the training?" Lipika asked the trainer as they sat in the living room.

"Not bad. He's a well-behaved dog."

"How many days of training does he need?"

"Around two weeks should be enough."

"Alright."

"I will see you tomorrow at the same time." The man's gaze stopped at me as I was peeking from Mummy's room, and he gave me a wicked smile.

Oh, boy... he's coming back again. The thought was frightening. I had to get rid of him, but I didn't know how.

Next day was business as usual. It was morning, 8 a.m., and Nikhil was leaving for the office.

"Manish, shall I drop you to your college?" Nikhil asked.

"No, *jijaji,* you go, I have an assignment to submit, so first, I will be going to the library," he replied.

"Lipika, are you ready?" Nikhil asked.

"No, I am working from home today. My whole team decided to work from home today," she said.

"Lucky you! Bye, Mummy," Nikhil said and left.

I was getting ready for my walk and giving signals to Lipika by pacing the door. But then, I sensed the same unpleasant presence, and my worst fears came true.

The doorbell rang, and he came inside. I ran to Mummy. She was sitting on the easy chair, and I hid behind her.

"What happened, Oreo?" Manish asked me. I howled in response.

"Are you excited for your training?" He questioned.

Uh oh... I stopped howling immediately, wishing he could understand my language.

I crawled inside Mummy's *saree*, startling her.

"Oreo! What are you doing?" She asked while getting up.

In desperation, I ran inside the pantry and hid behind my safe place—the wheat flour tin. I was hoping they would not find me this time as well.

"Why doesn't he want to go? He loves his walks," Mummy asked the trainer.

"It's nothing to worry about. Dogs get extremely apprehensive about training. They all initially resist it," the trainer explained. "He'll eventually get over it."

"Oh, okay." Lipika said and came to the pantry. My safe place was not safe anymore. She leashed me and handed it to the trainer.

The same cycle of sticks and shocks followed. I was too scared to turn my face in any direction other than forward, lest I get hit. Once back, I again ran and stood beside Mummy.

"He is shivering, see his legs," Mummy said. "He is scared of the trainer."

"Why, Oreo? What happened? Training is for your own good," Lipika chimed in.

Yeah, try taking shocks daily, and then we'll talk, I thought angrily.

The next day, when the trainer came again, I felt helpless. I ran to Mummy's room and hid behind her. When called, I moved further into the room to seek safety.

"He refuses to go," Mummy repeated.

Lipika turned to the trainer and said, "He doesn't want to go."

"It's okay, this is very common. We shouldn't give in to their wishes too easily," the trainer insisted.

But when Lipika saw me whimpering, she made her decision. "I'm not sure about it. Let's stop his training for now. I will pay you for two days. Once he's older, we'll give it another shot."

Oh, what a relief it was to hear those words! They felt like music to my ears!

I broke free from the clutches of the trainer. I had to show him that I was free. So, once the front door shut behind him and the trainer left looking displeased, I barked at him from the window until I could no longer sense his presence.

However, it wasn't all play for me. I had a lot of work to do around home. The house was enormous and with a huge terrace. Once the episode of the trainer was a distant memory, I spent my days on the terrace chasing birds. I also had to keep watch to prevent other dogs from coming near our house. If any approached, I barked loud enough for them to run away.

Whenever I sensed a dog outside our house, I alerted the family by barking and headed straight for the door to guard it. If the main door was locked, I would run back inside to find someone to open it, usually Lipika. She accompanied me outside and supported me if there were multiple dogs on the street.

Lipika is an agreeable companion that way. She also helps me chase flies. Yeah, that too was my responsibility. If I detected any fly inside the house, I tried to catch it. Sometimes I succeeded, but most times, it flew past me. Lipika would come with a towel and push the fly towards me. She always helped me catch the flies, yelling, "Oreo, look there. It's heading to your right," or "On your head, Oreo."

And this way, we would spend hours chasing flies and birds.

Chapter 5

June arrived, bringing scorching summer temperatures across India, soaring above 40 degrees Celsius in most parts of the country—except in my birthplace, Bangalore. The city's delightfully cool climate offered a soothing respite from the sweltering temperatures. On one cool early morning, during my deep sleep in the early hours, I heard a doorbell.

I jumped out of bed. Who could it be at this hour? Just as I approached, Lipika rushed down the stairs, full of cheer and smiling, beating me to the door (it was the first and *only* time she beat me at anything).

As I ran behind her, she turned to me and sternly commanded, "Oreo, sit!"

When Lipika opened the door, she exclaimed, "Chhoti!"

Oh, the girl with the specs! I remembered from the portrait. As a new member of the household, I was excited to make a friendly introduction. With my tail wagging and my bum swaying, I eagerly awaited a warm welcome. However, to my surprise, Chhoti entered the room and reacted with a startling intensity.

Upon seeing me, she executed an impressive, Olympic-level leap onto the sofa, her agility and speed making it clear she was highly startled. Her reaction was so dramatic, it seemed she could have earned a gold medal for her performance.

"Oreo, stop!" Lipika called out, trying to calm the situation. Turning to Chhoti, she said, "Chhoti, get down, he won't do anything."

But Chhoti's fear was palpable. "No, I don't want to be anywhere near him. I am scared of dogs! If he's going to be in the house, then I won't stay here," she declared, her voice filled with distress.

I heard her, then snarled, making her jump once more.

Who is she? I thought, looking at her. She is so thin that if the wind blows too strongly, she will fly away with it, and yet she has the guts to say I need to leave! No, truly; the girl was maybe sixteen, or even younger: a tiny frame, specs on the face, and though it was a cute face, it was red with anger.

"*Kya hua*?" Mummy also came out of her room hearing all the commotion.

Seeing Mummy, Chhoti's dramatic behaviour escalated further. "Mummy, I am going back to college right away. Please ask Manish to book my ticket," she cried out, her fear overshadowing her ability to stay calm.

"I dislike him."

"Chhoti, calm down!" Lipika urged, trying to diffuse the situation.

"Why did Nikhil *jijaji* get him? Send him to a different home," Chhoti demanded with frustration.

Unaware of the reasons behind her dramatic actions, I watched as Chhoti spent the rest of the day jumping from sofas to beds, visibly distressed. It was as if her fear transformed her into a whirlwind of movement, avoiding any contact with me. When she needed to use the bathroom, Lipika tied me to the window. Yes, she tied me just so that this girl can roam. That was unfair, and my non-stop barking made sure they got the point.

Did no one tell her I don't eat humans? I am not a savage dog! I tried telling her this by howling and wagging my tail, but the faster my tail wagged, the louder she screamed.

Well, I also have self-respect. So, after vying for her attention for a while, I moved away and sat on my bed. I observed her when she wasn't paying attention. She wore spectacles, and I like people with specs; they seem to have four eyes, which I find funny. I noticed her sneaking cautious glances at me.

I ignored her and got on with my busy routine—chasing birds from the terrace, taking Nikhil and Manish for walks, making Lipika happy by eating food, inspecting Mummy's room, chasing street dogs away, wagging my tail at every passerby, and most importantly, keeping my bed warm. Is my job hard or what?

After a few months, we had another visitor, Prabalika. I felt her calmness the moment she entered the house. She didn't touch me at once because she had a terrible experience with our species. One of us bit her when she was just two years old. But she didn't create any fuss, jump on sofas and beds, or voice any dislike for me or hatred of dogs. She simply walked in, kept her bags down, and looked at me.

"Hi, Oreo. How are you?"

I wagged my tail in excitement.

"No, Oreo. Stay away," Prabalika commanded calmly when I tried jumping on her.

"Come in," she said to someone behind her as she kept her luggage, "he won't bite you." Then, I saw him—a towering figure with broad shoulders and an imposing army-built physique. He carried a large stick in his hand, holding it defensively, almost like a shield. Despite his formidable appearance, he moved slowly and deliberately, clearly scared of me.

"This is Brijmohan." Lipika introduced him.

Though he did not jump on the sofa like Chhoti, he was walking close to the wall to avoid being in contact with me.

"Why are you so scared?" Lipika asked him.

"Look at him, he is just a six-months-old puppy. Once you look at him, you will fall in love. Touch his brown fur, it is so soft. If nothing else, look at his eyes; see, he is so innocent," she continued.

"Prabalika, you can touch him as well, he likes being petted. Look into his eyes!" She was like my faithful ambassador.

Soon, the family exited the living room, including me, but Lipika was still doing Oreo-*puran*.

The next morning, Chhoti came into the living room and immediately plugged her nose.

"What is this smell?" She questioned with a grimace.

“Oh, Oreo, you smell so bad!” She said, moving further away from me. That was insulting.

I am clean. Every time I came from a walk, either Manish or Nikhil wiped my paws with a cloth. I got brushed every week. And then I even went to dog spas for deep brushing. Maybe she’s the one who is stinking and thinks it’s me.

“Do you guys not give him a bath?” She asked Lipika.

“We brush every week and deep brushing every month,” Manish said.

“We haven’t given him a water bath yet as he was sick and very young,” Lipika said.

Water bath? What is that? Maybe another type of brush. I was trying to understand what my human family is trying to do next to me.

“We should give him a water bath, he smells so bad,” Chhoti said.

“Let me ask his vet first,” Manish said.

Next morning when I came back from the walk, they did not wipe my feet, but tied me to the gate and went inside. I saw two buckets filled with water kept on the veranda. There was a bottle of shampoo. Lipika came out with two towels in her hand.

“Oreo, it’s bath time.”

“Oreo, come,” she said, untying me from the gate and moving me towards the veranda.

Chhoti was there as well, watching the spectacle. I looked at her angrily. She is the one who started it all.

“Get the mug,” Lipika commanded Chhotti.

She did as told, then Lipika put the first mug of water on me.

As soon as the first drop of water trickled down my body, my heartbeat rose, and I started trembling. For me, being subjected to baths evokes feelings of discomfort, reluctance. The water was cold. I tried moving away from the bucket, but Lipika pulled me by the leash.

"How soft your fur will be!"

"You will smell like lavender, Oreo!" As if I cared if it was lavender or rotten eggs! To be honest, I would have preferred the latter.

I started howling for help.

The cold water would have frozen me if not for my gal, Prabalika, coming to my rescue.

"Why is he crying so much?" She asked, touching the water. "It is so cold. No wonder he is shivering." So, she commanded Chhoti to get some hot water.

After a few rounds of Chhoti going back and forth from the bathroom, my water was lukewarm. Though I still disliked the sensation, this was much better than cold water.

Once the shampoo was all washed off from my body, Lipika towel-dried me. Prabalika exclaimed, "Oreo, you are bleeding!"

She bent down and examined my whole body for any cuts.

"Oreo, you have a cut on your front paw." She ran inside and got me a bandage. She wrapped it around my cut. See, I told you; my kinda gal.

"Oreo, you get a treat for being so brave," Lipika praised.

Finally, I was allowed to come inside the house and was greeted with a big bowl of milk, which I gulped up fast!

Chapter 6

I enjoyed the vegetarian meals with my family; they tried to make them diverse, with menus shifting from curd-Cerelac to curd-rice, bread-milk, milk-carrot-Cerelac and apple-curd. But I always craved my native diet. Every evening during my walk, the enticing aromas of boiled eggs, fried chicken, and fish curries made me want to jump fences and reach for them. I longed to be inside those houses.

Our house stood next to a kind uncle who did not like dogs. Every morning and evening, he chased away stray dogs with a baton, shouting, "*Gallech*, go away!" I felt satisfied with this as it lessened my task of keeping dogs away from our street. He never shooed me away, though; he would stand beside our fence and chat with me.

One thing about his house I found most appealing was the distinct scent of cooking fish. The aroma was astonishing, and I couldn't understand why at times my family kept our windows shut and shielded their noses. God, these people don't know what they were missing. I would stand at the stairs, sniffing. His kitchen window opened towards the stairs, and his house was grilled on the sides. Often, I would try to part the grills using my paws, but they won't budge. Every time fish was being fried or chicken cooked, I tried, but the iron railing never let me pass through to uncle's kitchen. Well, you win some and you lose some. This one, I surely lost.

I had embraced my destiny of being a vegetarian and contemplated taking *sanyas* from food, becoming an ascetic, and living a life of solitude and devoid of any pleasure. But then, the unthinkable happened. One evening, returning from my routine walk, I detected something divine near my house—a waft of wind carrying an aroma I had never noticed in my house. The aroma of boiled eggs. I ran inside. In the foyer, what I saw made me jump with joy.

Manish was squatting, a newspaper spread out before him, and a packet in hand. I reached towards the cover.

"I have a surprise for you!" He said, showing me the egg, the white oval beauty glistening in his hand. The shell was smooth and flawless. I jumped and sat near him, waiting to see what came next! My mouth watered.

"Oreo, you are drooling! Just one more minute," He laughed, and I watched as he gently cracked it open, the delicate sound of the shell breaking filling the air. Slowly, the vibrant golden yolk emerged.

I had difficulty maintaining control, but I waited patiently as Manish took out four boiled eggs and started peeling them one by one. He fumbled, peeling one small piece at a time. A novice. It would be faster if he rolled the egg on paper and cracked it beforehand.

But I exhibited patience. One by one, he broke and mashed the eggs, both the yolk and the white.

"Oreo, come. Your eggs are ready!"

I was waiting for that word—'come'. Without hesitation, I gobbled up the eggs in just two minutes, relishing every bite and ensuring not a speck was left on the ground. It was a proud moment as it marked my first independent meal, and I was delighted with my accomplishment.

"Wow, Oreo, you ate so fast! We didn't even realise," Manish commented, impressed by my speed and enthusiasm.

"After all, it's eggs," Lipika acknowledged, understanding my omnivorous nature. Then, there was a discussion about the appropriateness of feeding me a diet that aligned with my natural instincts.

"Yes, true. He is a meat-eater by nature. Why should we convert him to vegetarianism?" Manish questioned, advocating for my dietary preferences.

"That is our choice. Why force it on him?" Lipika chimed in, emphasising the importance of allowing me to eat according to my natural instincts.

"I will get him boiled eggs daily from the restaurant," Nikhil offered as a solution.

Discussions about the nature of beings and the food chain continued for some time, but I drifted off to sleep after my heavy and hearty dinner. Since that day, Manish got boiled eggs from the restaurant every day, and I ate them by the door. The eggs never made it to the kitchen; I had them in the foyer. It didn't matter to me where I ate, as long as I got my eggs.

Soon, an electric egg boiler appeared in the house, and they used it to cook my eggs in the living room. It was fun, despite Papa scolding them. Boiling my eggs and giving them to me became a daily ritual, and I loved being part of it!

Meeting Papa was an exciting experience, and of course, worth sharing.

A few months back, when I first saw him enter the house, I noticed a white disc positioned behind his head, emitting light, which made me think a yogi had arrived to bless me. As he entered the house, I realised it was just the sunlight creating that vision. Jokes aside, he is the most religious person I have ever met, and he inspires positivity all around himself. When he came in, I immediately jumped on him, checked his luggage, and began my usual routine when someone arrives home.

"No."

I ignored him as my curiosity got the better of me.

"Oreo, no! I need to take a bath. Stop it, *beta,* there is nothing in the luggage."

I simply don't understand how people can not enjoy a dog jumping on them. He didn't pet me, he just touched my head once and said, "Enough now." He is rigid with his rituals, forbidding any touch after bathing or entry into his *pooja* room. But as you all know, I am my own master. I would lie quietly on my bed and pretend to sleep. When Papa emerged from the bathroom and headed to the *pooja* room, I would grasp his *lungi* and refuse to release him. He would get so angry with me. I wanted to try to play and have fun. Sometimes, I would lie in the *pooja* room and wait for him. I just wanted to give him company, but to be honest, I also enjoyed teasing him! He used to travel a lot for his work, so whenever he was home, one of my tasks was to sit with him when he did *pooja* and pull his *pooja dhoti* after his shower.

"What is this smell?" Both Nikhil and I were startled to hear such a loud noise. We were in the foyer, as I was waiting for my eggs while Nikhil peeled them.

We both looked up to see Papa with a suitcase at the gate. He was out on a tour.

"Why is the house smelling rotten?" He growled again.

"Nothing, Papa, we are just giving Oreo his eggs."

"Eggs! Now we have non-vegetarian food coming inside a pure vegetarian house? A house where we do not even eat onion and garlic?" He was aghast.

"*Kya kya din dekhne pad rahe hain,*" he lamented.

"He can eat what we eat. Why do you have to give him eggs?"

"We have never even stepped inside a non-vegetarian hotel, and now you have eggs inside the house," He lectured, covering his nose.

"*Kya hai,* Papa. It is his diet, he needs proper nutrition," Lipika countered.

"There are dogs who live well on vegetarian diets too. Nothing will happen if you do not give him eggs. Dogs happily eat whatever you feed them." Papa reasoned back.

"But we should feed him according to his dietary requirement, not what we want him to eat," Lipika retorted. "We all eat whatever we want to eat; no one forces us to eat against our will, then why should we force Oreo from eating according to his instincts?" She continued. "He is our responsibility, Papa. He is dependent on us. We must understand his likes and dislikes and feed him accordingly," she blabbered on.

"But vegetarian food is good for his soul," Papa opined. "We are eating so, and now it's proven you can get enough protein on a vegetarian diet as well."

"But Papa, we are vegetarians by choice, but we are forcing him. That is not right," Lipika countered again. "If he refuses to eat eggs, we will gladly give him a vegetarian diet. But as of now, he is running after them and gulps them in a minute."

This back-and-forth banter continued every evening between the father-daughter duo, while the rest of the household watched in amusement.

Despite the ongoing banter and disagreement, Manish or Nikhil reliably ensured that I received my eggs each day, regardless of whether the family reached a definitive decision on the matter or not.

Chapter 7

Just over a year into living in this house, I experienced a blessing. While standing on the first-floor balcony, I saw her—a tiny, pure black creature scouring for food. My first thoughts centred around the sight of a stray dog on my street. Where is uncle? Why isn't he out with his stick chasing her away? I needed to act. I started barking. That's when she looked up, and I met her jet-black eyes, matching the colour of her hair.

She had an inquisitive demeanour and a sharp nose that could detect the faintest of scents. It was sleek and slightly pointed, always twitching at the slightest whiff in the air. Her ears perked up at every sound, and her eyes—bright and alert—seemed to absorb everything around her. Her sleek, fur-covered body was built for agility, and she moved with a graceful, almost stealthy confidence. She indulged in the dog food my family had left out. I hadn't finished it last night. They never threw my leftovers; instead, they left them outside for the strays, against my wishes. But today, I felt pleased. I ran downstairs, taking two stairs at a time, and dashed outside. She was busy finishing up the leftover Pedigree, and I got busy looking at her. Her scent drew me closer. I had to meet her. But I knew that if I asked my family, they'd never let me out. What does a tiny, lovesick puppy do?

Find a way and improvise.

So, I looked around, but the fence was too high for me to jump. The gate remained locked despite my efforts to push it open. Then I noticed the space in between the grills of the gate. I was tiny and had a thin frame. I attempted to wiggle my body through the grill bars, and I did. Where there's a will, there's a way. I was out!

She noticed me, panicked, and started to run. I started running after her. I caught her as she entered a broken pipe on the side of the road. Our eyes met, we sniffed, and I swear I heard violins playing somewhere. She ran again, and I chased her. She acted hard to get, but I didn't quit. How hours flew by in this game of thief-police, we never noticed.

"Oreo..."

"Oreo!"

"Where are you?"

Voices of Lipika, Manish, Nikhil, Prabalika and Chhoti echoed in my ears. They were looking for me. I exited the pipe and saw them running from one street to another, calling me non-stop. I debated what to choose—love or family. When I looked back at my family, they all looked sad and panicked. I couldn't bear it. I came out of the pipe.

"Oh, there you are," Prabalika spotted me.

"How did he get out?" Lipika asked.

"It is possible someone left the front gate open," Prabalika muttered.

"Not me," Manish said.

"Me neither," Lipika said.

"Could have been the courier guy," Lipika added after some thought.

She lifted me up and brought me back. Being snuggled in her arms was not a terrible deal, either.

First love is tough to forget, and my relationship was only beginning to flourish. The next day, she was back. I saw her near the garbage bag that uncle had left outside his house. She sniffed it and tore it open. *Something worth looking at,* I thought, and ran towards the door. I sneaked out through the bars.

From then on, it became a regular occurrence. Either my Blackie (the name they gave her) jumped the gates to come inside the house, or I would slide in between the bars unless the main door was left open, and we would run on the streets. When thirsty, water from the drain quenched our thirst. When hungry, leftover food from dustbins gave us energy. It was an era. During that time, we were two unrestrained spirits fearlessly facing the world.

Every early afternoon, I would find her lurking outside our gate, waiting for me to get out. Rain or shine, she was there, waiting, nibbling on my leftover Pedigree. She would keep glancing towards the balcony, maybe for a glimpse of me!

I sensed that my family disapproved of my love life. They always pursued me, chasing after me just as I would chase Blackie. As soon as I slid out, no matter how quietly, they would know and start running after me. I let them chase me for a while, then I would get into the drain pipe or construction pipe with Blackie. They would stand outside, waiting for me to come out, luring me with praises and treats.

Most times, I showed sympathy and got caught. They never scolded me; I mean, not *never* exactly. Once, I received a good thrashing. Manish ran after me as I pursued Blackie. Being faster and smarter, she jumped across the streets and disappeared. I ran after her, only to find myself in front of a car. I wasn't fast enough. The driver braked in time, and Manish caught me in his arms. Back home, he slapped my face.

"You could have died! Are you insane? Don't you have everything? What is your problem, Oreo?"

"He manages to run away even when the gate is locked!" Nikhil exclaimed.

"Where does he go out from?" Prabalika asked, examining the fence. "I think he squeezes out from the space between the grill bars," she asserted, finding the escape route.

The slap did not hurt as much as the fact that they had, at last, figured out my escape route. Without wasting another second, Manish and Nikhil got to work. The front gate grills were sealed with horizontal wiring. A mesh material made sure I could no longer snuggle out. I patiently waited while they worked, sitting with them the whole time. I kept thinking about some other ways to escape. I was confident I would find a way one day.

After that, I had to content myself with just looking at Blackie from afar. Once I was sitting on the balcony, observing her jumping fences (she is the most skilled fence jumper ever!) and that's when I had an idea—I would learn from her. Every day, I would wait for her to come to my street. By this time, her attraction for me had also grown. When I was not able to get out, she would come in front of my house daily and jump inside our fence. She would call me outside but all my escape routes were closed for now. She was able to jump, I was not. But I observed her closely when she did this, noting how her front legs landed after the jump and her posture before the jump. I took in all the details. But I was scared to try it myself. I have never jumped a fence before, and it looked like something only my Blackie could do. One day when she was inside our fence and my family came to chase her away, I saw her more closely when she readied to jump. The key was in bending the knees. She bent her front knees, then stretched the hind legs: that is what gave her the force to jump. Now I was also ready.

Confident that I could no longer run away, my family again started leaving the front door open. As I sat on the veranda, my gaze fell upon Blackie, who had just arrived. She howled, calling out to me. She was running in the direction of our hideout. I realised she must have found a nice treat there. I had to get out, so I reached the corner of the house where I had seen her jump. I saw confidence in her eyes, which encouraged me to take the leap.

Voila! I was out; I was free again!

On this occasion, we wandered for hours before my family noticed my escape. We were back in our game of cat and mouse—I would escape, and they would chase me without fail. In hindsight, it kept my family healthy, running after me daily. Even their health was becoming my responsibility, you see!

Chapter 8

The house in Byrasandra, Bangalore, was where I experienced my first auto ride, and it remains my favourite form of transport to this day. Although we had a car, Mummy did not like troubling anyone. So, whenever she had to leave the house, she'd call a three-wheeler that would make a lot of noise. And then, one day, I finally got to sit in it.

When an auto came and stood in front of our door, I started pacing around the house, thinking Mummy was departing for somewhere or someone was visiting. Since I didn't sense anyone entering, I knew she would be going out. But to my surprise, Nikhil arranged a bedsheet on the seat of the autorickshaw.

"Oreo, come," he called. My joy knew no bounds—he was taking me along!

We gave the auto driver the address. Nikhil entered the auto first, then I followed with Manish sitting on the opposite side. Once inside, I attempted to leap onto the seat, but it was too narrow to stretch my legs. Squatting, too, was difficult so I jumped to the floor and stood between Manish and Nikhil's legs. This was much better.

I stuck my face out of the enormous open gate and enjoyed the wind. I loved being squeezed between two people whom I loved the most with my face in the wind and my tail wagging in the open air. I loved the ride, and my family noticed my happiness.

"He likes it," Manish observed with a big smile on his face.

"Yes, he really does," commented Nikhil.

"Oreo, we are going to visit the new vet," Manish chimed in.

Lipika was right; the old vet, though good, was more inclined towards medicating. On every visit he would give me some injection or another. Lipika, on the other hand, was not very keen on over-medication and believed in a holistic approach. So, she wanted to try another vet.

After an hour, the auto stopped near a temple.

"Sir, we reached," the driver confirmed.

"We are at Ragigudda Temple," Manish said, coming out of the auto.

"This definitely is not a veterinary hospital," Nikhil laughed.

"But this is what you told me, 'Ragigudda, Banashankari'." The driver was perplexed.

"*Bhaiya*, this is Ragigudda Temple, Jayanagar. We said 'Ragigudda Road Banashankari'," Manish explained again.

"I cannot go again. Give me my money and get another auto." He was angry for no reason.

“But why? You should have confirmed if you were confused,” Nikhil said.

“Yes, you never asked which Ragigudda, and we thought you knew where Ragigudda Banshankari is,” Manish added.

“Sorry, but I cannot go. I need to go home.” The driver finally accepted his mistake. Nikhil paid him, and the three of us exited the auto. Manish called another auto; we reached the hospital just as it was going to close.

The actual doctor’s visit turned out to be uneventful as it was just a routine check-up. He gave me a clean bill of health.

The journey back home proved even more delightful. By then, I had become a skilled rider, standing by the gate, drooling as I watched two-wheelers, three-wheelers, and four-wheelers whizz past us. People on bikes gave me a second look, glancing at the auto rickshaw in their rare-view mirrors before turning back to smile at me. I wagged my tail at double speed in response.

I reached home, tired, but happy, and met with the rest of the family to tell them how joyous I was.

From that day onwards, whenever an auto came to my house for any of my family members, I’d take a ride first before they left.

“He really loved the auto ride,” Nikhil said, amused.

Every evening, after returning from office, Nikhil would call an auto and take me for a ride around our neighbourhood. It was our alone time. Just me and him. With the soft wind brushing against my face and the warmth of the setting sun, I was in pure bliss at those times. The aroma of delectable chicken from the restaurants, and the sight of stray dogs made it undoubtedly a joyous experience for me. Seeing me drool in front of the chicken shops, Nikhil one day did the unthinkable.

"*Bhai*, stop here," he told the auto driver. I was ready to jump out, but he tied me to the railing of the auto. He went to the shop of my dreams, from which the smell of meat drifted. I was appalled. He left me and went all by himself. I barked for him to stop. But he just smiled and went inside.

After some time, I saw him come out with a packet and a water bottle in hand.

"*Bhaiya*, is it okay to eat non-veg in your auto?" He asked the driver.

"No, *bhaiya*, no eating food."

"Can you take us to a park then?"

He sat inside the auto and started moving again. The smell from the packet was hypnotising me. We reached near a park, and Nikhil pulled me outside the auto. He did not need to pull me out actually, I jumped.

"Oreo, wait, this is for you only," He claimed as I was trying to snatch the packet from him.

"Let me remove the excess salt."

He took the chicken out of the packet, cleaned the fried pieces with water, then placed them in front of me. I took one bite, and I was on the moon. This was nothing like anything I ever ate. To my surprise, he gave me all the four chicken pieces he got and did not even take one bite. I was really touched by his gesture.

"Oreo, this is our secret, just me and you!" He said as we were riding back home.

Back home, I slept contentedly after having the best meal of my life.

"Oreo, your egg!" Lipika called me.

"What happened, you are not waking up even for the egg?" She asked again.

"He might be tired from the auto ride, give him time. He will eat later," Nikhil said. I looked at him, and he smiled at me. This was our secret.

I would give anything in life to stay like this. But time inevitably shifts, and mine did too. Nikhil left home right before I turned two. With bags packed, he left in the middle of the night. I howled and howled for him, but he did not come back. Those days were incredibly tough—I couldn't even eat. Whenever Lipika or Manish brought a bowl, I turned my face away.

"It is okay, Oreo, Nikhil has gone to the USA. He'll come back during vacations." Manish tried to console me.

"Why are you worried? We are there *na*. We love you, Oreo," Lipika added.

But no words could cajole me out of my misery. I yearned for Nikhil. The days passed slowly and painfully. But as they say, time heals everything. With my family and Blackie's support, I fought to rebuild my life, only to face another setback.

A few months later, I noticed a flurry of activity in the house again. They packed bags and did a lot of shopping, which always put me on alert. In my two years with this family, I had learned that increased activity either meant someone was coming or going. Soon, at midnight, a taxi stopped in front of our house, confirming my worst apprehensions. Enormous bags were loaded, and I began pacing the house—someone was departing once more.

It was Lipika.

She sat down beside me and said, “Hey, Oreo. I am leaving for the USA, buddy. But I will come every six months to meet you. I promise. Always remember, I love you,” Lipika said in between tears.

She can be extremely emotional at times. Anyway, as soon as I realised Manish was not going, I felt better. But she kept on crying as she bade goodbye to Mummy, Papa and Manish. Even after she sat in the taxi, I could hear her sobs. Mummy and Papa also cried. They had a very emotional send-off.

The next morning, I missed her terribly. As usual, I had expected Lipika's non-stop chatter, but the house remained unusually quiet. It felt like mourning, prompting me to take matters into my own paws. Ignoring my loneliness, I started leaping onto sofas, showering Manish with kisses, and tugging on Mummy's *saree*, encouraging her to play with me.

I heard a thumping sound on the door, and thank God, Chotti came. Her entry changed the entire atmosphere in the house. She embodied a more mature version of Lipika and brought with her a ton of energy.

“Rishika, *tu*?” Mummy exclaimed in astonishment.

“Yes, Mummy, surprise!”

“I didn't know you were coming!”

“Mummy, that's what a surprise is,” she smiled. She turned to me and said, “Oreo, my darling, how are you?”

Yes, she was no longer jumping on sofas to avoid me; we were friends now!

I jumped on her and licked her in response. She stayed with us for a week, and we enjoyed a lot: playing, going to the terrace, chatting (she, just like Lipika and Prabalika, was very talkative!), and chasing away crows and squirrels.

Life resumed its rhythm, with me spending time at home with Mummy. Manish left in the morning and returned in the evening. He took me on walks after coming home. After dinner, he lay in his bed, and I lay beside him. We would fall asleep within minutes—Manish tired from his office and house chores (helping Mummy with grocery shopping and cleaning the kitchen) and me from taking him on our walks, guarding the terrace against crows, chasing away the stray dogs, and just being me.

I got used to Mummy always being at home with me, so her leaving for vacation one day devastated me. Only Manish and I remained in the big house. She left with Rishika in the evening, with bags and suitcases, telling me she'd be back in fifteen days. I wondered how I would manage those days by myself in the house. This made me anxious. I was scared. When they left, it was evening, so I could find solace in Manish's presence.

The next morning, when Manish left for the office, I found myself alone in the house. I never enjoyed being alone.

Before he left, Manish had said, "Oreo, I am going to the office, okay? I'll come back at lunchtime to meet you. It's just a matter of four hours. You eat food and rest, okay?"

His words didn't comfort me. As soon as he left, I started pacing the house, looking for my family. I knew they weren't present, but I kept on searching, checking closets, under the bed, and in the bathroom. There was no one. I ventured into the *pooja* room, crying and whining to God for compassion. When that didn't work, I tried sitting in Mummy's room on her bed. Her scent provided some comfort, but before long, my agitation resurfaced. I ran out of the room, climbed on sofas, ran up the stairs, searched the upstairs room, and climbed on the dining table. In my panic, I peed on the sofa. I usually take pride in keeping the house clean. I never pee inside the house; even in the dead of the night, I will make sure to go out to relieve myself. I was pacing the kitchen, trying to find comfort in my safe zone behind the wheat tin, but to no avail. The more I howled for peace, the more I felt my stomach growl. Before I could even realise, I found myself pooping on the kitchen floor. I tried to clean it with my paws, only to find myself making the house all poopy with my stained paws. Now I was stressed about getting scolded as well. It made me more stressed. Stress increases stress, believe me.

With my constant howling, my throat dried up, but I had no wish to drink water. I continued to scream. Finally, after hours, I resigned. I sat on the floor by the entrance, waiting for the door to open.

I heard the key click and stood on all fours as Manish walked inside. I howled once again, my tail wagging furiously with immeasurable delight.

"Oreo, how are you? See, I promised you I'd come back at lunchtime. Let's go,"

We entered the living room, and he halted.

"Oh, my God! Oreo, what have you done?" He was talking about the shredded cushion and torn newspapers scattered inside the house. He stumbled into the kitchen, his jaw dropping in disbelief. "Oreo!"

I braced myself for an earful. But to my surprise, he sat in front of me.

"Oreo, it's okay. You don't have to be so worried. We'll always be there for you. No matter where we go, we'll always come back." He patted me on the head and said, "Now go sit on your bed. I'll clean the mess."

As I made my way to my bed, he called out from behind, "Oreo, I'm sorry for leaving you alone. Tomorrow, we'll find a way, so you won't feel so, okay?"

I had to pinch myself. Is this guy for real? I messed up the house, and Manish didn't even raise his voice. I am really lucky to have him in my family.

Manish spent over an hour cleaning the house, picking up waste, wiping the floor, and mopping. Only then did he eat his lunch. He didn't return to the office; instead, he took half a day off for me.

Manish took out his phone as I was sitting in my bed, playing with my toy and said, "Roop, *yaar*, I need a small favour."

"You are free during the daytime, right?

"Can you come home and stay with Oreo, please? He is scared because he has never stayed alone before, and Mummy won't be back for a few days.

"He messed up the entire house today in a few hours, and I cannot take off." Manish was anxiously pacing the hall while listening to his friends.

"Thanks, man. I owe you big time," he sighed with relief.

I was touched again; he is making sure I am not alone when he goes to office. It literally brought tears to my eyes; I'm so lucky to have him in my life.

No, I am a big, brave dog, and I am not scared of anything. It's just that I dislike staying alone. They are two different things. Are we clear?

The following morning, Roop *bhaiya* came. I had met him before. His scent resembled that of a German Shepard. He exuded a great deal of kindness, letting me sit beside him on the couch with my head resting on his lap (yes, he allowed me to do that), while he remained occupied with his laptop. Soon, I drifted off into my dream world.

When Manish came back from the office, it signalled party time. They took me for a walk, cooked their dinner, boiled my eggs, and we chilled out in the living room. Three boys, living life to the fullest.

Life became enjoyable again. I embraced change in the pursuit of happiness.

Chapter 9

I came into the world with wheels on my paws. Having already changed houses twice, I embarked on another life's adventure. Growing up in Bangalore was just a small part of my life. My real-life adventures began when my brother Manish got married.

One day, right from the morning, I sensed something was happening. Mummy was bustling in and out of the kitchen, cooking up a storm. The sisters were busy tidying up the house. We usually do such thorough cleaning during Diwali, or when we are expecting someone important. I sensed something exciting was about to happen. When they tied me to the window in the evening, I was certain someone important was coming. I felt a rush of excitement.

In the evening when I returned from my walk, instead of letting me free, Manish tied me to the railing. And that is when I realised—someone new is coming. Whenever a new person comes, I would be tied up. Otherwise, I am always free. Later in the evening, a pretty girl, along with her parents, walked inside the front door. The second she saw me, she jumped. I was shocked by her behaviour. She screamed and leapt back, out of terror. I just wagged my tail, tied to the window as she hesitated to enter the living room. I was saddened to see her tremble like a leaf.

Lipika came forward, hugged her, and took her inside. "Oreo won't do anything. He is very friendly," she explained.

I kept calling the girl, trying to tell her that I was harmless, howling and growling. I wanted to know her better. After all, she would become the wife of my brother, the person I had shared a bed with for the past couple of years.

I had responsibilities. Yet, she was anxious. I thought, *well, we'll tackle her after marriage,* and lay down on the bed. Whenever she glanced at me, I stared at her. People might claim that I attempted to intimidate her. And who knows, they could be right. I'm neither denying nor accepting anything. No comments.

Chapter 10

Activity in the house intensified after a few months. Daily, the three sisters and Mummy would go out and return with bags of stuff, mostly clothes.

They all had arrived at our Bangalore home and were staying for some time now. How long and why, I didn't bother. I was just happy to have everyone in the same place until the time I heard their discussion.

"We need to start booking tickets for Agra."

My ears perked up; they were visiting Agra, the place of Taj Mahal! Excited is an understatement of what I was feeling. I will visit *the* Taj Mahal!

"We need to decide on Oreo's arrangements when we go to Agra," Prabalika suggested.

What! What arrangements for me? Am I not going with them? Will they leave me and go? I got up from the bed and sat next to them. I am as much family as they are.

"How about dog boarding?" Lipika asked.

I looked at Lipika in shock. Only she can think of leaving me in dog boarding. I moved away from her.

"But he dislikes staying alone," replied Prabalika.

My gal, my sister. Only she thinks for me. I looked lovingly at Prabalika. In response, she kept her hand on my head.

"He won't be alone. There will be other dogs for company," Rishika chimed in, looking at me.

She stretched her hand to pet me. But I moved closer to Prabalika. Rishika is not my sister anymore. I looked at her angrily.

"Yes, we'll find a suitable place for him, one that provides good care," Lipika added.

"We can, but we all know he would rather be with us than anywhere else," Prabalika muttered with concern.

I was touched by Prabalika once again. She is always thinking about me and really knows me. I would rather be in a ditch with my family than on a gilded yacht without them.

Lipika said, "But it will be too long a trip for him to Agra."

Who is she to decide? Am I deciding if it will be a long trip for her and so she should skip her brother's wedding? Then why is she deciding it for me?

These discussions became very common during those days as the family weighed the pros and cons of all viable options. They first decided to keep me in dog care.

One fine day, an autorickshaw got summoned. I was loaded in, and we left. The route stayed the same as the one we took to my vet. I assumed we were going for my check-up again. We reached the vet, and he took me inside.

“Look, Oreo, this will not be bad. I will pick you up in the evening.” Manish was consoling me on the way.

“You can even make friends here,” he said.

As we made our way inside the clinic, we went right, instead of our usual left to one of the check-up rooms. The right pathway opened into a large room filled with crates of all sizes, housing animals like dogs, cats, and a few rabbits. The dogs got alert seeing me and started barking. Never the one to be undermined, I barked back, and they stopped first. The area was dimly lit and had a noticeable odour of urine. I tried to mark, but the attendant denied me. Instead, he took me to a crate a little bigger than my size and pushed me in.

“Oreo, no need to worry. Have fun,” Manish said, petting me. He kissed me on my forehead and then the attendant closed the door of the crate. After a minute, he turned back and said again, “I love you, Oreo.”

I knew he was trying to reassure me, but the moment the door shut, shivers ran through my body and my legs quivered as if experiencing an earthquake. When I found myself confined in the small cubicle all by myself, I realised I wasn't just left alone in the crate, but in the entire room. I started trembling badly; I was so distressed that I peed in the crate itself. I had to get out. I banged on the crate door. I had to get to my home and my family!

“Oreo... Oreo! What happened?” Manish rushed back to the room on hearing the noise. He petted me through the gate and then turned to the attendant.

“I am taking him out of the crate,” Manish declared.

“It's common for them to act like that at first, but they adapt. Don't worry, sir,” the attendant explained.

"No, no! Take him out right now," Manish commanded.

"You will still have to pay," the attendant said tersely.

"I never said I would not," Manish retorted, then opened the crate gate to take me out.

"Oreo, come on. Let's go."

Happily wagging my tail, I stepped out. While casting a glance back at my fellow beings, I sensed a mix of envy and longing. I left with Manish, feeling a touch of sadness. The doctor, like many before, called me over-pampered. But my family kept doing what I wanted. I had trained them well, after all.

I have issues with dog care centres. I dislike them. Period. While preparing for Manish's wedding, my family tried not one, but three dog care centres.

Following the incident at the veterinary board house, my next visit was to an exclusive dog boarding centre. By exclusive, I mean it encompassed dog-boarding and nothing else. The centre was significantly larger than the room full of crates I had seen at the vets. It was also much cleaner than the vet's horrible stinking room. Each crate contained a bed with toys inside, and the attendant seemed friendly here.

Manish left me, departing before I could cry. I suppose he was trying to be smart. The attendant took me inside the room filled with crates. They had ample space between them, with a food and water bowl in each crate. All the dogs here were silent. Yeah, not a peep from anyone. What a bore, I swear.

They put me in one of the crates. But I am not naïve; I stayed quiet till they gave me treats, food, and took me out for a walk. But as soon as they locked me in the crate,

I made sure they realised my discomfort. I started with whimpering, but when that did not help, I increased my volume a tad bit. My howls, in mere minutes, motivated the silent dogs to join me. Before long, the entire centre resounded with howls. It seemed like everyone had now remembered what they were missing. It was a joint meditation session, community howling therapy.

I am uncertain of the events that followed, but within an hour, around 1:00 a.m. in the night, my crate opened, and someone discharged me. I noticed Manish standing there in his PJs.

"Oreo, what happened?" he asked, still half asleep. He sighed loudly and added, "Come on, let's go home." As we made our way outside, he mumbled, "You could've managed one night here. It's a nice place, Oreo. But no, you had to create a ruckus. Do you even know what time it is?" he kept blabbering, but I kept ignoring him.

I simply wagged my tail in response, and off we went home. I was a happy dog that night, sleeping with Manish on his bed.

My family was slow in grasping my point. Despite these incidents, they failed to understand my desire to attend the wedding. I wanted to be with them. Alas, they tried again. They considered that dog care might not be good if dogs were in crates. So, they considered open dog parks in lush areas, with large grounds where dogs roamed free amidst nature instead of being kept in crates.

They made a few calls, set appointments, and finally called the autorickshaw again.

"Oreo, you will like it here. It has more space than our house. You will have a lot of area to roam."

That day, even Mummy came with us to drop me. The drive seemed endless. We passed city traffic, moving onto narrow roads covered with trees on both sides, and then through fields of paddy. We passed herds of cows grazing in the lush green lawns, and just as I thought we would never make it, we reached our destination—a huge double-storey building surrounded by wire railings on all sides. The building had a large front yard where toys like Kong treat buddies and tug ropes lay scattered. Despite my resolve, I liked the place. A few dogs were roaming around the wire fence. We visited the owner, and later, I enjoyed the area and the spaciousness amidst the many dogs playing. It seemed fun as long as my family was with me. While Mummy and Manish sat on the chairs, I started playing with other dogs. We barked and jumped at each other—all in good fun. We played tug, they gave us treats, and I relaxed, looking forward to a good day.

"He seems to have settled here. *Chalo*, let's go."

Manish took Mummy to the main gate, and I saw them getting in the autorickshaw. I howled and whimpered to let them know I wanted to go back. But they left, and I disliked that. I do not appreciate it when things go against my wishes. But don't underestimate me, I have a knack for ensuring they go my way.

Because of my non-stop whimpering, they tied me to a leash. This offended me further. As you know, I am a smart dog. So, I got to work and, having chewed my leashes many times earlier, I had become somewhat of an expert in freeing myself from any kind of leash. I got to work silently and diligently. With persistence, within an hour, I was free.

I started towards the fence and tried getting out. Most of the areas along the fence resembled a mesh, posing challenges for navigation, but in one corner, there was a large enough gap for me to slide through if I attempted a military crawl, which is exactly what I did. I left and started running towards my house. I wanted to catch the auto, but a rotten odour from the right diverted my attention. As soon as I decelerated, I was apprehended. Before I could understand what had happened, I found myself confined in a room. My anger grew so intense that I yelped uncontrollably. I resorted to chewing on their toys in frustration, and when even that didn't bring any relief, I attempted to bark and intimidate the other dogs. In an instant, a cacophony of sounds erupted, escalating into a massive war of noises. As expected, within an hour, I found myself on my journey back home. This time, my family paid more than just the daily charge. Well, not my fault. I never asked them to leave me.

"We had to pay a fine of 5000 bucks, Oreo! You did a lot of damage there—chewed off two leashes—not one, but two of their toys, *and* their fence. You are a riot!" Manish shouted.

"Leaving him in dog care is becoming way too costly," Lipika chipped in.

"He will never stay there. He has already made it clear," Manish commented.

Finally, they got my point. I don't enjoy being away from my family. After that, they never tried keeping me in any dog care.

When the wedding time arrived, I was to go with the family. Conversations around me resumed, with the focus shifting from dog care centres to my travel plans.

"Flight will be easier; it takes less time," Lipika said.

"Yeah, but they sedate dogs before putting them on a flight," Manish countered. "Roop's dog got an ear infection after travelling by flight."

"Because of the change in air pressure?" Lipika asked.

"Yes."

"Train, then?"

"Train will take two days, and he cannot travel in normal coaches."

"Do we need to book first class?"

"Yes. It will cost much more than the flight itself, but it will have to be first class only."

"But I have a friend whose dog travels with her on a flight in her seat itself. No sedation." Chhoti suggested curiously.

"That's for smaller dogs, Chhoti. Had Oreo been smaller, we could have taken him with us. But they don't allow bigger dogs with the passengers," Prabalika explained.

"They sedate the bigger dogs and put them along with the luggage," Manish chimed in.

"And that's what is giving me anxiety. We can't have him sedated, not if we have other options." She turned to Manish and said, "Train will be better for him. Don't you think?" Prabalika added.

Manish pondered on this for a second before adding, "Let's take him by train."

So, it was decided.

"But who will accompany him?" Prabalika asked.

“Papa will be coming to Agra later than others. He can bring Oreo,” Mummy said.

“Even my leave begins late, so I’ll also come with Papa and Oreo,” Manish said.

“*Arey waah!* Oreo is travelling with the *groom!*” Lipika exclaimed.

“*Sahi hai*, he can be your protection too. Oreo, make sure you get our groom safely to the wedding,” Prabalika joked.

They reserved the tickets for a first-class coach, and we set off. For the first time, I felt joy as luggage was being packed. This time, even my toys were being packed. Two autorickshaws were called on the day of the journey, yet even they couldn’t accommodate our luggage. We had ten enormous suitcases (packed with clothes, I’m certain) and five bags. My bed, food, and water bowl were packed as well. Rishika accompanied us during the journey too. After boarding the autorickshaws, we departed for the railway station; Manish and I in one, Rishika and Papa in the other.

After about forty-five minutes of manoeuvring through the infamous Bangalore traffic, we reached the railway station. It was bustling with activity. There were so many people, and everyone was in a hurry. I felt taken aback by the quantity of luggage; every individual was carrying at least two of them. I looked around, mesmerised,and realised every family was carrying at least twice as much luggage as their size.

We had to first book our luggage as, apparently, we had much more than the ‘normal’ amount. Manish unloaded the items at the heavy luggage counter, and I followed him. He hadn’t asked me to follow him, but I pulled hard until Papa took me where Manish was. I must take care of the groom, remember? He's fortunate that I was there. Another thing I noticed at the station was that there were a multitude of stray dogs in the area. When I saw a couple of them approaching, I stood next to Manish and began growling.

"Don't you dare come near him or any of my family members," I told them in our language.

They were brats and began barking. I barked back too, louder, and growled too. I got ready to strike, my two feet firm on the ground, and front feet ready to jump if they moved even an inch in Manish's direction.

"Shoo, Shoo... Go away," Papa stepped in, although it was unnecessary. I was fully capable of defending my family. All the dogs left after Papa shooed them away, but I would like to believe that it was also because they feared me. Anyway, I kept guard.

After Manish finished the formalities, we all collected the remaining luggage and made our way towards the platform where our train was expected. The platform was packed with people and even more luggage. They sat on the ground with bed sheets laid out. A few were walking around holding a cup of tea, coffee, or different snacks. Mothers ran after their kids, either providing them with food or begging them to stay still. Several people were perusing the bookstalls. There were a few dogs here, just a couple at the end of the platform. We kept our luggage in a pile and waited for the train. The platform appeared clean, but the tracks were a veritable treasure. Lots and lots of garbage, ranging from poop to bones. I contemplated getting rid of my leash and jumping onto the tracks but right then I heard a loud whistle that made my bones shake.

"Oreo, our train is here. Rishika, you hold Oreo. Papa and I will get the luggage," Manish declared.

"Oreo, come here," Rishika called me.

The train had barely stopped when people started making a beeline for the gates to enter the bogies. Everyone attempted to enter the train at once. Seeing them made me feel as if I was being left behind, so I pulled hard on my leash and tried to get inside. But before I could make my way inside and secure seats for my family, Rishika stopped me by holding firmly to my leash. I went to her and sat alertly beside her. We stood and watched as Manish and Papa loaded our luggage in.

Finally, we walked towards the train. I noticed there were two steps leading into it as the train stood higher than the station. I had assumed it would be a cakewalk, but it turned out to be difficult as the stairs were too narrow. I thought about it for a second before directly jumping in the coupe. One jump, and I was inside the train!

Our compartment resembled a small cabin with a door and four seats, two above and two below. Before anyone could claim a seat, I jumped and took the bottom left seat. White sheets were spread out across all the seats, and each one had a blanket and a pillow. On my seat, Manish spread my blanket on top of the white sheet. I still wonder why! Anyway, I nestled near the window, even though observing the outside world was challenging because of the window's opacity. While I got comfortable, the rest of the family arranged the luggage and filled my water bowl. With a book in her hand, Rishika climbed up on the other bottom seat and Papa followed suit. Manish, as expected, sat with me.

"Oreo, you comfortable? This is your home for the next thirty hours, buddy," Rishika said.

I responded with a small bark and settled in further. When the train started, the rhythmic motion lulled me into sleep, and I entered my dream world. After some time, a sudden jerk startled me. The train had been moving at a slow pace, but now I could sense it gaining speed. I had to position myself firmly to avoid falling. I thought the movement would stop eventually, but it did not. It took some time to get used to the motion. I felt uneasy for a while. I was sceptical about eating anything as I knew that if I ate, I would hurl it out. Manish offered me treats, but I didn't take them for fear of throwing up.

By evening, though, I had grown used to the movement of the train. I figured out that if I didn't resist the inertia of the motion, it felt fine. I swung along with the train, not making any effort to stop myself, and that strategy proved successful.

I stretched myself on the bed again and slept. I had a simple dinner of curd and rice to avoid stomach issues. As the day changed into night, the train kept moving, sometimes slowly and sometimes at the speed of a bullet. It stopped at periodic intervals, and I kept waiting for its stops, as it meant a walk for me on the platform. Venturing into unfamiliar locations, marking them, and returning to the train before other dogs could apprehend me was exhilarating.

"Oreo, it's time for a walk," Papa said as soon as the train stopped at another station.

"Hurry, Oreo. We're only here for five minutes," he commented hastily, putting on his shoes. I jumped from my seat, ready to be leashed and taken out. Others roaming in the passages made room for me, and within a minute, I leapt onto the station with Papa.

We walked towards the exit to avoid the crowd and hawkers. Vendors shouted at the top of their voices.

"*Chai...*"

"*Garma-garam samosa... Jo ek baar khayega woh baar baar aayega...*"

"*Poori ley lo...*"

The hawkers covered the length of the train, walking alongside the windows, luring people into buying their stuff.

"*Le lo, madam. Bache ko accha lagega,*" one of the vendors was trying to sell a toy car to a child's mother. When he spotted me, he ran and approached Papa. "*Sahab, ye ley lo... Bohot soft hain...*" He held a white stuffed rabbit in his hands. I started wagging my tail so hard that the onlookers wondered if it might just fall.

Papa saw my enthusiasm and asked the vendor, "How much?"

"Only twenty rupees. Take it, *sahab*, your doggy will be very happy." The vendor played his masterstroke and knew it would work.

I wagged my tail even more to support his claim. Four minutes later, we walked back inside our cabin with a white stuffed rabbit hanging from my mouth. I jumped in my seat and started playing with it.

"Wow, Oreo! New toy?" Manish asked me.

"Papa... you never bought anything for us!" Rishika complained.

She was very much like Lipika; she never grew up. And now she wants my rabbit! I clenched the rabbit tightly between my teeth, in case she tried to pry it away.

Every station the train stopped at from Bangalore to Agra now bore my mark. As soon as the train slowed again for another stop, I would get out of my bed and be ready by our cabin door to exit. The stops were too short, and I barely got much time to mark a few spots. So, I would get started on my business as soon as I alighted from the train. On stepping onto the station, I would first take in my surroundings. My first targets were the trees, dustbins, and other frequented spots by strays. Once finished, I moved on to the next target, such as stairs, flower pots, and other similar places, if time permitted. I would continue my work right up to the last second, when the train would whistle loudly to announce its departure, and then I would quickly return to our coach. By evening, I had mastered this routine.

Although I enjoyed getting down at the stations, the trip felt like a never-ending journey, and I felt bored. We spent one entire day and night on the train, and although I took short walks at the stations, it was nothing like my daily two-mile walks. I exercised caution and only consumed curd during the journey. My stomach remained unprepared to consume anything else.

I tried stretching on my seat, sitting, and watching the scenery outside the window whenever I felt bored of playing with my rabbit toy or sleeping, but I couldn't discern anything as the windows were too blurry. Objects passed by us, trees, buildings, villages, schools, and buses, all swept along in our wake. I tried opening the windows with my paws, but it didn't work. I only ended up hurting myself. Someone had sealed them shut.

As I was busy figuring out what to do next, Papa kept himself busy with his *pooja*, *jap*, and reading religious books. Rishika remained engrossed in some book while Manish slept. But I wanted to play, so I clutched my torn rabbit and took it to Manish, putting it on his face.

"Oreo! You have covered me in your saliva," he said wiping his face.

I wagged my tail. I took the rabbit from his hand and started jumping around with it. Despite the limited space, I fit in between the seats, which were only a foot apart.

"He is getting bored," Rishika said, getting down from her throne. She pulled another toy from my bag and threw it at Manish. I ran up to him. Instead of giving it to me, he threw it back at Rishika. I might have done two such rounds when I caught hold of the tail of my squirrel. And then I pulled on it till Rishika relinquished control.

The tug of war lasted for about an hour, leaving me parched and famished. I had my first solid meal of boiled eggs (Manish got them from the pantry) and drank water. I fell asleep to the rhythmic movement of the train, which worked as a lullaby.

"Oreo... get up!"

I woke up as Rishika barked in my ears. I observed that the train had arrived at a station. I thought it was time for a walk, so I quickly got ready.

"Oreo, wait," she said, holding onto my collar.

Why did she wake me up if she wasn't taking me for a walk? I had been running across miles of green fields towards a roasted chicken. She had a knack for doing this—she'd never let me reach the chicken, even in my dreams.

The train started moving again. I felt a jolt of anger; she not only disturbed my sleep, but did not even take me out for a walk. Now she was asking me to wait.

I looked around the empty cabin. Where were Manish and Papa? It was just the two of us in the cabin. Even our luggage was gone.

Oh, dear God! No! Do not leave me alone. Where is my family? I hurried towards the cabin door.

Chapter 11

"Wait, Oreo..." Rishika caught hold of my collar. She came out of the bathroom and caught me. "This is not our station. We will not be getting down here. Papa and Manish are going ahead to get the luggage. We'll meet them when the train stops at the next station," She explained to me as I howled at her. I sat near her. As the train started running faster and faster, I realised that Rishika was my responsibility now, at least until we reunited with Manish and Papa. I kept my head on her lap to comfort her.

After about ten minutes, the train stopped again. This time, Rishika picked up my leash in one hand and her bag in the other. After inspecting the cabin for any remaining luggage under or behind seats, we alighted. As soon as we set foot on the station, I caught sight of Manish and Papa. I pulled on my leash and guided her towards them.

As we stood at the station. I started pulling on my leash again, sensing the powerful presence of my fellow beings lingering in the area. I had to mark my territory. We roamed around for the next five minutes and when the train whistled, I ran towards the door of the train.

But Manish pulled at my leash instead of getting in himself. I howled, wagging my tail at him, letting my family know the train was going. But they stood there watching it go. They did not budge.

"Oreo, this is Agra. It's our station," Rishika said. She turned to Manish and suggested, "Manish, let's hire a coolie."

"Is the car here?" asked Papa.

"No, I called Prabalika, but they are stuck in traffic. We will need to get a cab," Rishika responded.

So, Agra was our destination. Hmm... a map would have avoided the confusion and the whole me-trying-to-enter-and-them-trying-to-stop-me drama. Man, these humans... They never learn, do they?

Just as I got used to the train routine, mastered marking, learned to entertain myself in a confined space and eat while moving, and began to think of the train as my new home, we moved again. I believe I truly was born with wheels on my paws.

As Manish and Papa went about finding the porters, and Rishika got busy on her phone, I was lost in my thoughts when I noticed people staring at me. The place was overwhelming, with people bustling about and bumping into each other without apologising. Everyone stared at me as though they'd never seen a dog before, especially one guy getting off the train. I felt uncomfortable and wagged my tail. Yet the people did not come near me; they just looked at me and laughed from a distance. They acted as if they had seen a miracle. Some were gaping at me, some were just standing, amused. One brought their son to show me. *Oh, hello! Have you ever seen a dog travelling in a train!* I wanted to ask them. After a while, porters took our luggage, and we left the station. Finally, I experienced comfort and calmness, relieved to be away from the staring people and the stressful environment. On my way to our destination, I had learned that Agra was my family's maternal and paternal home.

As we made our way out of the station with the porters carrying our luggage, I was surprised by the abundance of animals outside. The reality surpassed everything I had ever imagined till now. My eyes caught sight of herds of cows sitting and grazing on the grass, and the dogs having their own ongoing party right next to a huge dustbin. The roads were covered in litter and seemed to have more garbage than the bins, making it a perfect party spot. I felt tempted to explore the pile of garbage on the road too. I slowly inched my way forward, but a sharp tug on my leash stopped me.

"Oreo, stop! Come here," Rishika shouted.

I retraced my steps. Besides cows and dogs, I could see a strange animal on the road. They called him 'pig'. He sure looked funny, with his protruding mouth and bloated nose. They were rolling in the muddy water in the ditch by the road. They looked like they really liked dirt.

My family had a hard time getting a cab. Unlike Bangalore, people were not ready to give me a ride here. My family was getting restless, calling out to one cab driver after another, bargaining with autorickshaw drivers and cursing Agra, all at the same time. I didn't bother myself with their troubles and got busy checking out the surroundings, sniffing, and marking the entire station, this time from the outside.

If, and only if, all territories were determined by what I had marked, my family would have owned everything from Bangalore to Agra. They would have been filthy rich by now. But this world and its strange rules did not allow my family to own whatever I had marked. It seems like my markings had no value in the human world. Weird creatures, I tell ya.

One autorickshaw guy agreed to let me ride in his auto for an extra fifty bucks. Manish quickly loaded our luggage in my auto and said, "Oreo, sit," patting the seat of the rickshaw.

I jumped inside the auto, ready for another trip. It seemed to me like travelling would never stop. Manish accompanied me in my auto, and Rishika and Papa came in the other car with the rest of our luggage. The auto began its journey, and I started to feel hungry after having relieved myself two times already. As time passed and I breathed in the cool air, I began feeling thirsty as well. It felt like my stomach was waking up from its dormant state. I am nothing if not well-behaved, so I kept quiet and waited for us to reach home.

The roads here were narrower compared to Bangalore, and the traffic was horrible, even in the morning. The honking was worse as the bikers did not budge their hands from the horn.

"It is red! Why are the cars not stopping?" Manish shouted, and I looked up. All I saw was a brown light.

"*Bhaiya*, move. It is green for us now... wait!" He shouted as the auto stopped with a sharp brake. "Why did that side start moving now? Oh God..." Manish was clearly frustrated, but I was not able to understand it. Light was still brownish-yellow.

Maybe he needed an eye checkup? He was seeing something called 'red', 'green', and not sure what other colours, when the only light visible was brown.

After an hour of riding through the chaotic roads, the auto stopped in front of a big house.

I could see the rest of my family standing at the gate, waiting to greet us. I started getting down before the auto came to a complete stop.

"Oreo, no! Wait," Manish barked. "Wait until the auto stops completely."

My family always stops me from doing anything exciting. Anyway, I cranked my neck to get a full view of the house. It was a double-storey building, adorned with garlands. Smells of roses and marigold were wafting through the air, tickling my nose. They must have decorated the house for my arrival! My heart soared with joy, grateful for everything my family had done to welcome me to the family home. Well, I deserved every bit of it, and more.

I could not contain my excitement anymore. As soon as the auto came to a halt, I hopped out. I had to jump over Manish as he was still sitting, but it was fine. I know he didn't mind one bit. He knew I had to get down as people were waiting for my *swagat*.

Everyone was there: Mummy, Lipika, Prabalika, and Brijmohan. And Brijmohan was without his stick! That was new. Whenever he was around me, he always carried a stick because he was terrified of me. He's a doctor who fixes people's brains, but, in my opinion, he still needed to fix his own first. I am serious! Did he honestly believe I would fear a twig? Someone needs to tell him that I am a big, brave dog. I could have broken the stick in just one snap, but I let him think it scared me. He is the husband of my sister after all. I have to maintain cordial relationships with my extended family members as well, for the sake of my own family.

Once, in Bangalore when he was visiting, I hurt my paw with a glass during my walk and came home bleeding. He cleaned my wound (he did it without a stick), applied ointment, and bandaged it. He even gave me a tablet to help with pain.

The stick, I feel, was a way for him to defend himself. He *feared me*. His stick gave him the confidence that I would keep my distance. But little did he know that it was pointless. Didn't I tell ya? My family is crazy that way. But I still love each one of them dearly.

And then I sensed someone, someone I love the most. Then, I saw him.

My Nikhil!

I felt a shiver run down my spine... I was ecstatic! He was there too! I had not seen him for a year. He was standing there smiling with his hands resting on Brijmohan's shoulders.

I leapt and jumped on him. My Nikhil was here. He is back from the USA! He picked me up and hugged me tightly. We stayed there for a long time. Me soaking in all his scent and him nuzzling his nose in my fur.

Then I ran to meet the rest of the family. The luggage was still being unloaded, but I did not care to help. I went about my work, greeting each one of my family members with hugs and kisses. I was afraid my tail might fall off because of the intense wagging. That day, my tail had a mind of its own.

I licked them until they started to smell like me. Don't be mistaken, the wagging and licking is not something I do for myself. I do it for my family, to give them something to be happy about. They always get happy seeing me excited. It makes them laugh and giggle. So, I continue with this charade every time I see them.

The house was new to me, so I quickly went inside to make sure everything was okay for my family. Someone had to oversee the security, and if not me, who else? The ground floor had one room, a dining space, a living room, a bathroom, and a back porch. Everything appeared fine, no other animals were present, and I saw no markings from rival dogs. I climbed up to the first floor, leaping up two stairs at once. There were two rooms, two bathrooms, and a small gallery. Luggage from other members of my family, their clothes, and suitcases filled the rooms on the first floor.

I noticed the stairs did not end there; they went further up. There was a terrace! I ran upstairs immediately. There was a huge metal door. I tried to push it open, but it did not budge. I pushed again. Nothing. Then I noticed the lock. No wonder it was not opening. I dashed downstairs and started whimpering from the first floor itself. I went to Nikhil first, howled and whimpered, pleading for him to open the terrace door.

"Oreo, get out of the way; you will get hurt," Nikhil said.

"We are getting luggage, Oreo. Get out of the way!" Rishika shouted.

Rishika and Papa pushed me aside, but I persevered. I went up a few steps, then came bolting down. I approached Manish, glanced at the stairs, then back at him.

"He wants to go to the terrace."

"But he just came down."

"Is the terrace locked?"

"Yes..."

"That's why he is so anxious. He wants to go to the terrace."

Mummy gave a huge key to Manish and as he made his way up the stairs, leaving the luggage behind, I ran like the wind. I outpaced him, stood near the terrace door, restless. Humans took too much time, *precious* time. Those few minutes my family wasted in understanding what I wanted to do could cost us our territory.

Manish opened the door, and I rushed out. The terrace amazed me with its vast open space and rough concrete floor with only a water tank to break the surface. Concrete fences stood on all four sides for security. From the front side, I could see the park and its few trees and the fountain that adorned the centre. Houses flanked the other two sides. The terraces of the adjoining houses were touching ours. On the back side, an open ground led to a distant view of the Yamuna River.

You could see houses everywhere, big and small, including apartments, row houses, and villas. Trees were less abundant here compared to Bangalore, but there were huge fields with people working in them. A soft breeze was blowing, and the sounds of chanting were being carried on it from a nearby temple. The environment was spiritually ignited.

I saw my fellow beings here, roaming the streets. I could see tens of them roaming the street behind my house too. What the heck were they doing behind my house? I started barking. If the fence hadn't been too high, I would have jumped from the terrace. The hooligans were not deterred and carried on with their loitering.

I realised I wasn't dealing with the submissive dogs of Bangalore anymore. These dogs were more resilient and stronger. Their small size didn't diminish their commanding presence, urging me to strategise before taking any further action.

"Oreo, *chalo*. We'll come back later." I barked in response, and Manish added, "Do you not want food? You must be famished!"

Oh, yeah! Food shifted my focus. Deciding that I will deal with the dogs later, I resigned to the growing growls of my stomach and came downstairs. Bowl full of milk and bread, and Nikhil with a spoon, were waiting for me. After a very long one year, Nikhil fed me again, spoon by spoon. They had placed my bed near the stairs, and after I had my food, I relaxed on it. Even though the train ride was over a long time back, when I closed my eyes, I could still feel the rhythmic movement. I slept with Nikhil and Brijmohan sitting by my side, talking. I dreamt of terrorising those dogs, letting them know who the boss was.

In the evening, I went for my very first walk in the land of Taj Mahal. It was quite different. "Taj Mahal," Manish started, "is the ultimate symbol of love." Love! This word evoked so many feelings inside me. I could feel my heart flutter, and I remembered my first and forever love, my Blackie. Love also brought with itself the pangs of loneliness and pain of separation. That is what love is. Every emotion rolled into one.

To divert my mind, I focused on the surroundings we were in; practising mindfulness, you know? This land had its own vibes. The house we were staying in was on the outskirts of Agra. There was a lot of construction work going on around the neighbourhood and new apartments were being built everywhere.

We left our colony compound and walked towards the villages. Yes, there were a few villages next to our neighbourhood. I could smell the air filled with smoke coming out of the small houses and the fragrance of cow dung from the cowsheds. The area still had a fresh rural air, with acres of green fields on all sides. It was wheat and mustard season, and I saw fields covered in yellow flowers. It felt as if a huge yellow bed sheet adorned the ground.

A nagging feeling of being followed made me turn back and to my horror, I saw a horde of dogs following me. They were neither getting closer, nor moving away. They were thinner than the ones I had seen from the terrace earlier, but more vocal. They were not ready to accept my presence in their area, not even for a short walk, so they barked constantly. I tried to be the bigger person and remained calm, trying to concentrate on my sniffing. I was quite determined to finish my job. I was there to mark a territory for me and my family. Akbar once ruled here, and I wanted to be the ruler now. Such petty barks from petite dogs were not going to deter me. As long as they kept their distance, I was fine, and they did keep their distance because of the stick Manish was carrying with him. Unlike me, they feared the stick.

Narrow roads required me to navigate through the herds of cows, pigs, and donkeys. The road had more animals than vehicles! Some may not wait for another vehicle, but they patiently wait for cows and other animals to cross the road. And there were so many animals—cows, goats, pigs, donkeys, buffaloes, oxen, and dogs—it made me feel as if I was in a jungle and not alone. I felt one with them.

Manish and I roamed on the lush green fields of mustard. The path was muddy, and the crop fields lined the walkway, some growing corn, others wheat. Being in the natural village setting was very exhilarating, especially since it was my first visit. I immediately liked this life better than the city life.

We went through rows upon rows of wheat fields. It was green all around and the gentle breeze was making the plants dance in a rhythmic motion. I pulled Manish towards the fields.

"Oreo, the farmer will scold us if we get caught," Manish cautioned while getting pulled in my direction. In my opinion, he also wanted to explore as much as I did. We were roaming the fields and soaking in the sweet smell of raw wheat.

"Who is there?" A loud voice came screeching through the wind.

"Oreo, the farmer is here... Let's run!" Manish pulled me towards the road.

"Thief, thief!" That farmer had started shouting.

"Oreo, move! This is no time to face them." Manish pulled me hard. I was ready to face the farmer and tell him the truth.

But Manish just kept on pulling me and running towards the road.

We could hear the footsteps of people running towards the farm we were in. I looked back, and what I saw made me quicken my pace as well. They were all carrying huge sticks to hit us with.

Manish and I ran faster than Bolt, reaching the road in the nick of time.

"I know we should have told them we were just strolling. But they looked so angry, I thought running would be best," Manish explained when he caught me looking at him quizzingly.

Chapter 12

When I went to sleep that night, there were only nine members in the house including me, but when I woke up in the middle of the night, I counted more than twenty before me. I thought I was dreaming and slept again. When I got up in the morning, I realised it wasn't a dream! We had received a lot of guests overnight. The living room was filled with people, running up and down the stairs and, of course, their luggage. I got up and ran to greet all the new people, only to be pulled back. Damn it!

When I looked at the clock, I remembered they had forgotten my walk too. My food! Oh no... Where is my food? I panicked for a second before I saw my bowls filled with water and Pedigree. I exhaled a deep breath of relief.

"Oreo, you got up?" Prabalika asked.

"Did you expect me to sleep through the wedding?" I barked back.

"Who is this dog?" The source of the voice was an old woman. She was coming inside the house and was walking with a bent. She sat on the sofa and looked at me sternly. Her eyes were fiery. I slid behind Manish.

"*Bua,* he is Oreo. Our dog," Lipika said.

"Whoever he is... What is he doing inside the house? Dogs should not be allowed inside," she growled.

"No, *bua,* he stays with us at home only. He is our family," Lipika explained again.

"These new age philosophies. This is a wedding house. A dog crying and barking is not auspicious..." she continued.

"*Arey, Jiji,* let him be. He's the child of the house." At last, Mummy and Papa stepped in.

"We will keep him tied, so that he does not disturb you or the pooja," Papa said.

"As such, he never causes any disturbance," Mummy supported me again.

"Do as you wish," the lady said angrily and went inside.

"Why do we need to tie him?" Nikhil was protesting now.

"We cannot do anything else. *Bua* is the oldest, and even Papa is scared of her."

"We can take him upstairs so he can be in the room without being tied," Manish suggested.

"But when he is down here, he has to be tied," Papa insisted.

Well, besides the discomfort of constant bondage, the wedding proved very enjoyable. Few wedding guests petted me, took me for bonus walks, and fed me sweets I was otherwise banned from eating.

Yet one day in particular was horrible. Tied to the stairs, I was lying down on my bed, trying my best to sleep in the hustle and bustle happening all around me. A loud noise from outside made me jump on the bed. Someone was banging thousands of drums in my ears. Is it the terrorists? With bombs? Did they fire at our home? I had to save my family! I was used to paying close attention whenever Papa played the news. So, naturally, I was alarmed. No one was in the house. I had to act!

I tugged and tugged, but my leash wouldn't budge. I quickly set to work at chewing the leash. It took me ten minutes, and in that time, my heart was in my mouth. The sound was coming continuously, and the people were shouting outside the house. As soon as my leash tore, I ran out the door, ready to take on whoever was harming my family, the leash trailing behind me.

At the front door, I was in for another shock, my family was dancing right in front of the front door. I thought about it and looked at the drummers suspiciously. Maybe those drummers were making them dance. Who knows what they were up to? I ran to the drummers and started barking at them, warning them to back off.

"Oreo!" Prabalika shouted.

"*Bhaiya*, stop the drums for one minute," Lipika yelled.

Finally, the sound stopped. They heeded to my warnings.

"Oreo, how did you get out?" Lipika was perplexed. "Oh, my God! He ate his leash!" She was shocked to see my chewed-off leash.

"He might have been really scared," said Prabalika. At last, someone understood me.

"Yes, we should have been mindful about his sensitive hearing," Chhoti added.

"Wait, I will move him to the upstairs room, turn on the AC and shut the door and windows. That should help," Prabalika volunteered.

"Yes. That'll be much better. Oreo, *chalo*."

I tried barking at those drummers again, telling them to get out of the house, but it was to no avail. I howled at my family to come inside for safety. Instead, they shifted me, along with my bed, to the upstairs bedroom. Prabalika closed the door behind her after she got my food and water bowls, and fed me some treats.

I was really upset with my family. They were acting insane! They were dancing to the tunes of those drums. Instead of chasing those terrorising drummers away, they were inviting them inside the house. I could still hear them playing, but the sound was muted now. I guess they might have toned it down.

When I was just at my wits' end, they stopped. But the quiet was short-lived. Another commotion followed, this time inside the house. Everyone started getting ready. People were bustling in and out of rooms with clothes in hand. The girls were all giggling and talking loudly. Manish was being adorned with a turban, and people were jumping with excitement around him. Nikhil was applying *teeka* to Manish's forehead. Brijmohan was helping Manish wear *jootis*. Once more, I found myself speechless. Manish knew how to wear shoes. He used to take me for walks with shoes on, does anyone remember it? Why the hell were Nikhil and Brijmohan helping him wear shoes today? Humans and their peculiar behaviours are sometimes beyond my understanding.

Soon, the rest of the family got ready too. Papa and his brother took me for a walk. Prabalika got my bread and curd and fed me. Since landing in Agra, I had not seen eggs. Was this place experiencing an egg shortage? My diet here was milk-bread, curd-bread or Pedigree. I terribly longed for my eggs. I couldn't get them because I don't have a wallet or receive pocket money from my family. Unfair, right?

Slowly, the house started quieting down. And before long, Manish left.

With Manish, those drummers left too. The house was soon empty. I panicked. Where did everyone go? Manish had gone to get *bhabhi*, but what about the rest? And where did the drummers go? Were they responsible for taking my family somehow? Is this a case of abduction?

I started pacing up and down the house. The terrace door was locked, as was the front door. I tried the windows, but they were locked too. There was no way for me to escape and save them. I waited and waited and waited. No one came back.

After an eternity, I heard the front door open. Manish's cousin, Tanay, walked in. He was in a hurry, quickly went upstairs, took a bag and left. Saying nothing.

Was he responsible for my family's disappearance? What was in his bag?

I called out to him, barked at him, but he was in a daze, and left within ten seconds. No one else came that day. I was really worried. This was the second and probably the last time I peed inside the house. You know me, I never do it without a good reason. I have my ethics and rules.

All my treats, which Prabalika had left for me, lay by the side of my bed. Not a morsel would go down my mouth. I sat disheartened on my bed, waiting. After midnight, I heard a knock at the front gate. Alarmed, I ran to the kitchen window. I heard a few people talking outside. I ran and stood behind the front door, ready to tackle whoever it was.

I heard the click of the lock before the door opened. It was Prabalika. I was so relieved! Brijmohan followed her into the house. The only thought that flashed through my head was—they were safe. Finally, they could find their way back. But someone had to teach them a lesson. It wasn't right for them to leave me all alone in the house. I scolded Prabalika left and right, and she patiently listened to everything I had to say.

"Sorry, Oreo. We could not take you to the venue because it wasn't allowed." She cleaned up after me and then fed me.

"Manish is now married, Oreo. He will be coming in a few hours along with Prafulla, our *bhabhi*." She petted my head, and I felt myself relax under her loving touch. "The wedding is about to be over soon. We will have one new member in the house now," she kept on talking.

I paid attention to none of it. I knew she was blabbering out of guilt, so I let her, and pretended to listen as I was just happy knowing that they were safe. If she was here, the rest would follow soon enough. I drifted off to sleep. In the morning, my platoon was back, along with all the relatives. And I was back to my place, leashed next to the stairs.

Chapter 13

After the hustle and bustle of the wedding, the quiet was a welcome change. I was back to my routine of walking, eating, and sleeping. This was a new city, and I explored it inch by inch. It was very different from Bangalore, and I'd been itching to explore it *alone*. You know what I mean: no one tagging along with me. I believe it was normal for me to want to explore the world on my own, without a leash or someone holding the reins in their hands. It did not matter who held the leash. Normally, I was the one in control on my walks. I would steer them the way I wanted to, but sometimes, a guy needed to be alone on his walks to connect with nature and experience the deeper meaning of life. Right?

So, I started planning my escape. The front door was always open here, unlike Bangalore, but they always locked the iron gate, which was grilled like a box. The fences were a few feet high. As a novice at high jump, the fences were not an option. As the saying goes, "Determination always finds a way."

One late afternoon, there was a commotion at our front door. I woke from my nap and saw someone with bags at the door. I noticed the front gate standing open.

I shut my eyes again and pretended to sleep. If my family knew that I was up, they would have come to hold me. So, I pretended to be asleep. Both the doors were standing open, and Mummy was busy putting away the grocery bags in the kitchen. The delivery guy was waiting patiently by the front door for his payment as Manish went to get the money, and Papa was in the *pooja* room. The stars could not have aligned any better. I got up and within a second, bolted through the door at the speed of a bullet train and zoomed past the shocked delivery boy.

"Hey..." He moved aside the moment he saw me running his way.

"Oreo!" Manish shouted behind me.

I ran past the neighbourhood gate before Manish could leave the house. I was free! For the time being, at least. The first thing I did was to run off to the field. They never let me go into the fields. I was dying to see the paddy, smell the mustard flowers, and bask in the glory of the winter sun. Nah, I am kidding. I just wanted to mark my territory in the fields. This was the street dogs' hub, and I was dying to visit the place.

I entered the field, and there were five dogs standing in a group, ready to greet me. One of them, the pack leader I suppose, started barking. He took two steps forward. I did too. I even growled. We locked eyes with each other. Within a minute, he gave a loud bark and took a step back. Soon, others followed in his steps. They all barked and backed away together. Fleeing with courage? How funny!

This confirmed my suspicions about the dogs here being cowards. Or maybe their circumstances made them this way. Who knows what they had to go through? Being a perfect gentleman, I left them unharmed and quickly rushed to explore the other side of the fields.

My time was running out. I knew my family was out looking for me. I could faintly hear them calling my name. I took a mud road to the village. I had come here earlier with Manish and knew that Papa got milk from this area. I went around the houses and entered a few front yards, only to be scolded. At one place, a few children even threw water at me to scare me away. I dislike water. I ran like my backside was on fire. The children stood and laughed. But it did not deter me. I was on a mission to mark as many places as possible, and I did just that.

After forty-five minutes of running around, I saw Manish running behind me. He was breathless, but still persistently following me. By that time, I was tired, and his expression showed the same. I stopped and let him put the leash on me and take me home. I have to give it to them; they never scolded me.

Whenever they caught me, they just leashed me, took me back home, gave me water and then got on with their work. They neither scolded me nor praised me. I suppose this is what they mean by 'silent treatment'.

The first thing they always did was give me water before anything else. They cared for me so much that it was the reason that compelled me to run away more and more so that I could mark more properties for them. As much as I could! Although they were not interested in it, so much that they'd even tell me not to go outside at all, but I knew the law—to rule the world you needed to have the land under your jurisdiction.

Chapter 14

The morning after the wedding, a new person joined the household along with the other relatives. It was the same lady who had visited us in Bangalore, the one who had jumped back upon seeing me. No, not in joy, but in fear.

She stayed on the couch throughout our first meeting, never leaving the seat. Because of her, I had to be restrained all evening. I despised her back then. I had hoped that she would leave with the family friends but when that did not happen, I prayed for her to leave with the relatives. Unfortunately, all relatives had, but she was still there. She remained in our house even after everyone had left and only my main family remained.

I suppose this is what marriage is. She is a part of our family now and will live with us. I thought about it, and it upset me, as I had expected to be tied up for the rest of my life. But once the relatives left, I was left free. They did not tie me again. I kept up my part of the bargain and did not get in her way. I just went to her once, but when she hid behind Manish, I left her alone. I was already used to keeping my distance from Brijmohan, so what's another person? I could manage it for a few days, just for Manish's sake.

I thought I could easily adjust as it was just a matter of some time. But a few days later, she left and took Manish with her. I was upset and furious, but I had the rest of my family, so I managed to survive without him somehow. Nikhil and Lipika left next. The house was almost empty now. Mummy, Prabalika and Brijmohan left next. Only Papa, Rishika, and I remained. The house, once bustling with people and chatter, was now dead silent. Just when I had started to think Agra was going to be my new home, we packed our bags, loaded my bed in an autorickshaw, and hit the railway station again.

We were back in the train, in a cabin similar to the one earlier. My family never settled in one place, and they never let me settle either. Well, as long as someone from my family was there with me, I tried to be content. If I had my way, I'd always want to be surrounded by all of them. But I have no control over that. They keep coming and going without taking my permission.

The return journey was more comfortable, as I was already used to travelling by train by then. As soon as we entered the train, I jumped to take my window berth and started looking outside the window. When the train started, I saw stations, houses, and trees moving in the opposite direction. I could even eat this time. I was a professional now, always ready by the cabin door as soon as the train slowed.

It was great to go back to all the stations we had visited earlier and re-mark them all. To my horror, the goons had demarcated the territories I had marked earlier. It was good that we had come back. I think my family knew about this, that's why we were going back the same route so that I could mark my territory again, this time for good.

Chapter 15

The next morning, we reached Bangalore. Oh, the smell of my hometown's air filled me with indescribable elation. It was so good to be back. I cannot tell you how great the auto ride back home was. We had shifted to a new house before going to Agra. I kept thinking about it, my walks around the neighbourhood, and meeting my fan club. Oh yeah, though I never interacted with kids (they were too loud for me—always shouting and jumping; it was too much for me to handle), I had a fan club full of them in my neighbourhood in Bangalore. Whenever I went for my walks, the children of our new apartment complex would follow me around, shouting my name. They would walk with me, and the brave ones would pet me gleefully. Although I liked these little humans, they were too loud, and I was glad we didn't have any at our home.

When we reached home, I took two steps at a time to reach my first-floor house. My fan club followed me.

"Uncle, where did you take Oreo?"

"We haven't seen him in ages!"

"Was he sick?"

“No, we went to Agra for Manish’s wedding,” Papa explained to them all.

“How did he go to Agra, Uncle?”

“On the train.”

“Are dogs allowed on the train?”

They didn’t even know that. *How silly*, I thought. Bombarding of questions stopped after ten minutes, and we finally entered our house. I saw Prafulla standing in the kitchen. It blew my mind. *What* is she doing here? And *why* is she here? Where is Manish?

On cue, Manish emerged from the bathroom. I danced with joy. He joined in and danced with me. In the kitchen, Prafulla stood fixated, unmoving. Manish saw her, stopped dancing, and went inside to help her.

I looked at her again, she was smiling. I waited for Manish for some time and then went back to my bed.

During the night, I preferred sleeping with my brother. He was also used to sleeping with me. I was getting ready for the bed as usual; I had my walk, dinner, and now it was time to crash on the bed. My bed lay in the corner, but heaven forbid I ever slept on it at night. I would always sleep with my brother. I waited and waited… and then waited some more for Manish to open the folding bed for us. It was 9:00 p.m. already, and nothing along those lines happened. My family had their dinner, and everyone started wrapping up for the day and going to their beds.

“Good night, Oreo,” Prabalika said.

“Prafulla, you also sleep now. You must be exhausted!”

“Okay, *didi*,” she said and headed to Manish’s room. Manish was still watching TV.

He will open the bed after he's done watching TV, I thought. So, I waited. After switching off the TV, Manish came to me and petted me. "Good night, Oreo. You sleep now, okay?" he said, pointing towards my bed in the corner, and off he went into his room. The one Prafulla had gone to.

It wasn't hard to like Prafulla, but the hardest part was adjusting to Manish sleeping away from me. My bed was next to his door now. I could hear him snore behind the door, and that was comforting.

I'll knock on the door starting at 4:00 a.m. every day. Yeah, I know it is too early, but he needed to be reminded of our morning walks! You know if I wouldn't have done that, he would have completely forgotten about them. Well, everyone in the family is forgetful. I have to start at four in the morning, then they take me out by five. I'll start with a knock, then scratch the door. In between, I would take breaks, sleep for some time, and then again start the process.

"Oreo, five more minutes."

"Oreo, stop, *yaar*."

I felt appalled, hurt, and sad. You might have guessed by now how attached I am to my brother. Everyone says I am obsessed with him, but I disagree; it's just love and nothing else. Though that day, I realised that I was thoroughly unprepared to share him with anyone else. I continued waiting for him to return, open our bed, and sleep with me. Reluctantly, at half past midnight, I got up and went to my bed. Tired from travelling in the train, it did not take me much time to fall asleep. My last thoughts were about how to drive Prafulla out of the house.

Till now, I had been ignoring her, but not anymore. Before I fell asleep, I had a plan in mind. I had to get a few things in place quietly as my family wouldn't be pleased if they found out.

Next morning, I followed my daily routine as usual. After coming from my morning walk and having my breakfast, I pretended to sleep. I didn't go anywhere, not to any rooms, nor did I attempt to get close to Prafulla. I just lied on my bed and pretended to sleep.

"Oreo is very quiet today," Chhoti noticed.

"You're right. But why?" Prabalika asked.

"Maybe he's still tired from the train journey," Chhoti replied.

"Yeah, right. It must be taxing for him too," Manish reasoned.

"Let me check him for fever." Prabalika checked my ears, followed by my nose and paws, and proclaimed, "He doesn't seem to have fever. I think he is just exhausted."

They nodded, satisfied that I was fine, and left me alone to get on with their routine. After having breakfast, they cleaned up the kitchen and started preparation for lunch. Everyone had lunch in the afternoon; after tidying up again, they went to take afternoon naps.

I woke up and went to Mummy's room. Her loud snoring confirmed that she was in a deep sleep. Papa was still doing his *pooja*, oblivious to the world. I went to the next room. Prabalika and Rishika were fast asleep too. Books lay around them; they had slept off while reading.

Prafulla slept in the third room: Manish's. It was always open to me earlier, but since her arrival, this door remained closed. They had prohibited me from entering Manish's room. I slowly nudged the door, and it opened. It wasn't bolted. With one last check for movement, I quietly entered. Prafulla was sleeping on the bed, her hair fell down the bed. She looked so peaceful, so calm. I thought of going back. But the pictures of Manish on the night table reignited my resolve.

I went to Prafulla's side and sniffed her hair. They smelled nice, coconut and vanilla. She did not wake up. I inched closer. Her hand was lying by her side. I licked it once. Nothing happened. *She is a heavy sleeper,* I thought, and licked her hand again. Still nothing. I moved my face closer to her face. She opened her eyes, saw me staring right at her, and then...

She shrieked and jolted upright on the bed. Then she started crying and screaming at me. She ran out of the room howling. In an instant, Rishika and Prabalika were by her side.

"What happened?" Mummy was out of her bed too.

"Hmm? Hmm?" Papa was asking in sign language. He does not speak during *pooja*.

I was left standing in the room by the side of Manish's bed. Everyone was consoling Prafulla. They gave her water and asked her to sit down. Mummy and Rishika sat with her. No one came to me. I tiptoed out off the room and sat on my bed. Maybe now she'll go, and I can again sleep with Manish on his bed.

"Oreo, what did you do?"

"Why did you go into her room?"

Her room? No, it was my brother's room.

"It's okay, *didi*. I think he was looking for Manish. He just scared me, that's all."

Woah, wait a minute! Did she just take my side? I felt both shocked and ashamed. I still hoped that she would leave so I wouldn't have to stoop so low. If anyone asked me, though, I'd say I was only trying to get to know her better. I'm not saying anything else.

Well, she did not leave. Instead, she started talking to me. She would stand at least a few feet away and then start talking. The first time was when she was standing behind the safety of the kitchen counters. She had asked, "Hey, Oreo, you had food?"

I started rolling on the floor in response.

"Oreo? What happened? Are you okay?" Prabalika asked with concern.

I started chasing my tail, going round and round in circles.

Everyone started laughing.

"I get it. He is so excited that you talked to him, Prafulla," Mummy said.

Mummy got it as always. Prafulla stood there and smiled.

After that she was one of them, my sisters, I mean, non-stop talking, but she always kept her distance. She never came near me or petted me. Manish would beam with joy whenever he was around her, almost matching the happiness I had felt for my beloved Blackie. For Manish, I gave in and accepted her as a family member. She was gentle, with a soft voice and a pretty face.

Chapter 16

"Oreo, you are turning three!" Manish was talking like a three-year-old.

"What do you want for your birthday?" Prabalika asked.

"How about some chicken wings and pig ears?" I responded with an excited bark.

"Let's get him some chew toys?" Prafulla said in response.

I sighed... My family... if only they could understand me.

"Let's get him a dog cake," Lipika said.

"What is a dog cake?" Prabalika asked the same question I had.

"They make the cake with eggs and cheese and carrot, safe for dogs to eat."

Wow! Eggs and cheese, another two of my favourites! I was excited.

My family got to work. The house was decorated with balloons, which I had no interest in. Manish went out to get the cake. Mummy was busy in the kitchen making milk pudding for me and the family. I love her milk pudding.

"Mummy, you look pale? What happened?" I rushed inside the kitchen hearing Lipika.

"I am okay, just felt a little dizzy," Mummy said. "You guys finish the preparations. It's Oreo's birthday." She smiled at me.

"No, let me first check the sugar and blood pressure for you." Prabalika got the kits.

"Mummy, sugar is very high and so is the BP."

"We need to see a doctor; I will take an appointment," Lipika said and went out to make the call.

"We will go to the doctor tomorrow; today is Oreo's day," Mummy declared, and that was it. Everyone went back to their planning, but I could sense a little gloominess on the faces of the kids now.

Manish came back with the cake.

They put a conical cap on me, and then I was left in front of the cake.

"Oreo, go for it!" Before they could finish the statement, I was done with the cake. It was yummy.

I looked at my family once done, and they were all laughing.

"Oreo, you are covered in cheese!"

"Now it's time for the pudding," Mummy said, handing everyone a bowl. She also got one for me.

I slurped it down in one go as well!

It was a fun day, but struck with mom's health scare. For the next few days, I saw Mummy and Lipika going out to the doctors a lot.

"Her creatinine is rising."

"We need to see the nephrologist now."

"Will search for a good one this time."

Lipika and Mummy would leave with a stack of files in hand and return after hours. I caught Lipika crying on the balcony quite often. She would be bubbly and chirpy in front of Mummy, but sobbed when she went to put clothes to dry on the terrace. I couldn't comprehend it. If she did not like drying clothes, I wondered why she did not ask Rishika to do it? Rishika was visiting more than normal too.

In the evenings, Manish would return from work and would always bring something for Lipika and Rishika—their favourite cookies, *pakoras*, sweets, or coconut water. The four of us (Lipika, Rishika, Manish, and I) would huddle together upstairs while Mummy slept, whispering to each other. Prabalika would sometimes join us too, but she would often be travelling for work. Prafulla would also come for the discussions.

"Dr Istiaque is great, isn't he?"

"Yes, he is one of the best in the country. They discussed how Mummy's total liquid intake has to be reduced to half a litre." I was perplexed; only half a litre including milk, curd and water? I can never do that.

Her water intake had to be reduced to 400 ml in a day. They would alternate between whispering and crying, and I would just lie next to them quietly, looking at their faces.

"What happened, what did the doctor say?" sometimes Papa would come to ask, and every single time, the kids would give the same response.

"Theek hain, Papa. Aap tension mat lo."

Papa would always reply with a smile, "Whatever will happen will be good. God will do only good. Have faith."

But I did observe him spending more time in the *pooja* room as days passed.

A few days later, in August, I saw a truck stop in front of our house and gigantic boxes were moved into one of the bedrooms. *Someone was coming*, I thought. A few days later, Prabalika came to stay with us. This time, she came for good, leaving her job in Mumbai. A few weeks after Prabalika came, Lipika left for the USA. I haven't seen Lipika break down like that before. She cried all the way to the airport.

The house was gloomier now. Mummy was her jovial self, always laughing, but I could sense she felt more tired than usual. After coming from her regular outdoor visits, she started sleeping for longer periods of time. I sometimes caught her crying in her room whenever she was alone in the house. I saw each one of them crying, Manish in the bathroom, Prabalika on the terrace (just like Lipika did before her), and Rishika in her room. But they never cried together. They could have, right? In front of others, especially Mummy and Papa, each one of them acted brave and laughed loudly, but it was quite obvious that they were faking it. If you thought this was bad, wait until I tell you about what happened that December.

Chapter 17

Mummy was very ill. I could see that her face was swollen. One day, they rushed her to the hospital. She was there for weeks. Brijmohan, our in-house doctor, immediately flew in. The day they brought Mummy back home, I was frightened to look at her. She had changed; she had a big scar on her neck, a thick tube hanging from it, and her right hand had a big scar too. When she came in and I went to her, despite her condition, she petted me, and at that moment, I saw her cry in front of everyone for the first time.

"Oreo, *kaisa hai*?" she asked. "I thought I wouldn't see you again."

It was the first time all of them were crying together. I felt terrible that day and couldn't eat. But life moves on. In a couple of days, we all went back to our old routine. Every other day, Mummy would go out for a couple of hours with either Prabalika or Rishika. She would come back very weak and tired. When I'd go to see her in her room, I'd be sent away.

"Oreo, *abhi nahin, beta*. Let me sleep for now."

"Oreo, *Mummy ke room se bahar ja*, let her rest."

"She has just returned from her dialysis. Come later, Oreo."

Mummy would be too weak to even speak and would simply crash on the bed. I didn't understand what dialysis was, but whatever it was, it was draining her out.

I would go away as told, but after resting, Mummy would call me to her and pet me.

When she would get ready to go out again the next time, I would try to stop her by pulling on her *saree*. I would bark at her too. I tried to tell her that if it was so tiring, no need to go. *Please don't go*. Simple logic. Right? If you dislike a place, don't go there. But from my own experience of going to the vet, taking those injections, and being force-fed, I know that sometimes you have to do what is right for the body, even if you do not want to and no matter how much pain it causes. Sometimes, pain is the only way to health.

My family's life started to revolve around hospitals. I had also grown used to being alone in the house during the day. But one of them always stayed with me; only it wasn't Mummy anymore. Now Papa started spending more time with me. Since his retirement, he had been spending most of his time at home.

Just as I was getting used to the new routine, one day I heard someone at our entrance. I was with Rishika at home, and she had tied me up before opening the door.

I had to protect Rishika and the house and get rid of these people before Mummy arrived. It was my duty. But to my horror, they had already emptied one-fourth of the house. I barked and barked, but they didn't bother. One of them came and took my bed too, throwing it in one of the boxes in their truck.

Rishika was just standing by my side as the men loaded their truck with our stuff and kept telling me it was all okay. *Okay?* What was she saying? I thought it was anything but okay. Rishika is useless. If she hadn't restrained me, I would have stopped those men. By the time I had chewed through my leash (it was thicker this time), the men loaded the last box in the truck and drove away, kicking up a cloud of dust. The entire house stood empty. Despite the open door, I had no desire to run outside. I had to save my house. I ran to Mummy's room when Rishika removed my leash. It was barren. They took everything. I was both angry and sad. I barked at her for not stopping them.

I sat on the floor, dejected and angry at Rishika. The place that once felt full of life and energy was now empty. The home became a house. The warmth of the home left with its inhabitants, and I was left with loneliness and the fear of loss engulfing me. I could not even look at her.

"Oreo, what happened? It's okay, please don't be angry. We will be leaving soon too."

"*Arey*, why are you not looking at me?"

She kept calling out to me, but I kept moving away from her. If she came near me, I went to a different place. I waited for Mummy to come back. Only she could make this right again.

But she did not come. In the evening, an autorickshaw stopped outside our door. It had to be Mummy, but no, it wasn't her. Instead, Manish came and asked me to get into the auto. Rishika stayed back. I asked her to come too; I cannot leave any of my family members alone. But she did not budge. I kept waiting for her to get in the auto before I did.

"Oreo, *chalo*," Manish dragged me into the vehicle. It was the first time someone had to force me to hop in the auto. I sat reluctantly. As the auto started moving, I could sense that I was not going to come back to my house ever again. I looked back and continued glancing at the house, howling for Rishika. I was doubtful if I would see her again.

We passed the BTM neighbourhood, crossed the big flyover in our auto, and found ourselves amidst the greener part of the city. Cherry trees lined both sides of the road, and yellow flowers ornamented the street. The sun, peeking through clouds, waking up the sunflowers. Spring was in full bloom in this part of the city. A light breeze carried the soothing fragrance of flowers. The roads were wider, and the temperatures several degrees lower than BTM, probably because of all the greenery. We kept inching forward through the heavy traffic.

The traffic was the only similarity this area shared with the rest of Bangalore. Our auto took a service road, and we entered a residential neighbourhood. There was much construction work happening here. But an abundance of greenery and parks accompanied each complex, and the road was still in development. We halted next to an apartment complex with bright yellow walls. It was a multi-storey building. We got off at the gate, and the security guard took our names, including mine.

Yes! He took my name and clicked a picture of me.

Oh, he is going to show it to his friends. I am famous! Just when I started dreaming about a red carpet for myself, he handed me an ID Card.

He then opened the heavy iron gate for us. Our auto zoomed in through the gate and stopped in the basement, where there were cars parked all around. We stopped right before the lift. After paying the auto driver, Manish guided me inside that small, clean cubicle before we went up. I felt my heart beating faster; everything was new, a plethora of things to explore and an abundance to sniff. When I got out, my bed was the first thing I saw. Yes, there it was, lying outside the lift near apartment no. 106 along with the rest of the boxes. All the things taken by those robbers were here.

Okay, I thought, *so we are at their den. Thank you, Manish. I am ready to fight for our things with those goons.* I took the position beside Manish as he pressed the bell.

When no one unlocked the door, I barked loudly to alert them we were there for our things. After five minutes, I heard footsteps approaching the door. Someone was coming to open the door. My front legs positioned themselves to pounce, back legs balancing the stance. I prepared myself. The door creaked open, and I glimpsed Prabalika.

Prabalika? What was her role in this? Where is Mummy? Is she still in captivity? Without waiting, I dashed inside, taking Manish with me. When I put full effort, even the leash can't hold me back.

"Oreo, stop," Manish stumbled.

"Wait, Oreo..." Manish said as he tumbled inside with me.

I dashed from one room to the next, trying to find Mummy. Finally, I found her; she was sleeping in a bedroom. I let out a big huff of relief. She is there. Everything is okay. My bed is there too. Oh my, I cannot emphasise enough how relieved I felt upon seeing my bed. A dog is nothing without it!

I relaxed and waited for my breathing to return to normal. Then I started checking the house. The front door opened directly into the living room, which connected to the dining room and kitchen. It was an open floor plan. A small balcony was next to the dining room. The opposite side of the house had three rooms with attached bathrooms. The bathroom beside the living room seemed to be common. The kitchen led to a small dry balcony which housed the washing machine. While I was busy exploring the house, someone placed my bed in the living room. My water bowl and food were ready too. If only Rishika would return, everything would be perfect.

I wondered what she was doing at that empty house. As if waiting for this cue, Rishika walked inside. Never have I been happier to see her. I wagged my tail at her and jumped at her with such force that she fell to the ground.

"Oreo, *kya hua*? How come you are feeling so much love for me?" She asked, trying to get up.

"Stop, Oreo," she said when I started licking her face. She never liked that.

"You were the last one to come. He is happy to see you."

I felt a cloud lift from my shoulders on seeing her. She petted me, and I went back to my bed with content.

As my family got busy arranging the house, the three robbers who had stolen the stuff from my house came back. Before I could bark at them, they started opening up the boxes and arranging furniture. I let them do their job. After all, they were undoing the wrong they had done earlier.

Chapter 18

"Oreo, *chalo*. We have to go for your walk," Manish said, holding my leash.

I was fine not going for the walk today, as there was so much happening. But never to say no to an invitation, I jumped at the chance to explore the neighbourhood. This time, we took the stairs that led to a walkway, which was lined with small trees that wound inside the building complex. There was a wide enough pavement alongside the fence for sitting. Behind the building, a children's play area was located with swings and a basketball court. I was yet to find the dog's play area. I guess humans don't make them, do they?

A huge iron fence guarded the complex on four sides. There were other buildings coming up near our building. We circled our apartment complex before exiting through the front gate and passing the yellow security station. The guard's cabin was near our front gate. Sparsely furnished, it just had two chairs and a table. There was a cupboard I was most interested in, as it held the lunch boxes of the guards. No matter what time of the day I passed the cabin, it always smelled nice with aromatic flavours. Thankfully, that was the only area which was yellow.

The rest of the apartment building was white and grey. There was a vacant plot next to our building, and that is where I met my match. There was some construction going on. Believe me, I have not seen more hardworking people than the ones on that plot. They started early and worked till late in the night. They were staying in this locality in makeshift houses. I paid no attention to them as I continued passing the plot. I detected a unique scent but couldn't find its source. Just as we turned the corner, a ferociously enormous white dog jumped out at me. I had to take a step back.

He was twice my height. I guess he did not believe in warnings, because he never barked, never warned me to get away from his territory. He was there in the bushes behind the makeshift houses, waiting for me. Manish picked up a stick, trying to shoo him away, but he did not budge. Seeing no other choice, I took my stance. I believe in non-violence, so I began with barking. Without responding, he jumped at me again. This time going for my neck. If not for Manish, it would have been my last day on this planet. Manish came in between us. He pulled the dog away from me by holding his collar, and pushed him aside. The dog then jumped on Manish. I felt appalled.

Messing with me is one thing, but messing with my family is a whole different thing. *You just crossed the line, buddy*. Charged with a sense of protectiveness and duty, I lunged at him. He was double my size, but within seconds I was sitting on his back now. I would have bitten his skin off had Manish not yanked me away from him.

Why me? He was the one who started it. Manish pulled me so hard that he lost his balance, and in the next moment, he was on the floor.

"Ouch! Ouch! I twisted my ankle." Manish was limping, and his knee was bleeding.

I looked at Manish's hand, he was bleeding. *Let me get back at this stupid dog,* I tried reasoning with Manish. But he just kept hold of my collar. The dog was not willing to retreat. Manish was contemplating what to do next when we saw a couple run towards us.

"Tommy! Hush..."

The big dog backed down.

"Oh my God. We are so sorry. We were just taking him for a walk," the man explained.

"Without a leash?"

"Sorry, he is a little temperamental. Are you hurt? How is your dog?"

"Yes, a little. I will have to check Oreo for injuries. Please keep your dog leashed when you get him outdoors. He could have caused actual damage to us," Manish chided, a little irritated.

"Sorry, once again. He has been vaccinated, so please do not worry about rabies." They leashed Tommy and took him back.

"One more thing, please do not hurt him. It's not his fault. You should have not left him unsupervised," Manish told them thoughtfully. We cut our trip short and went back home. Manish was limping badly. He was in a pretty bad shape if you ask me.

"Manish, you guys came back so early?" Prabalika asked when she opened the door for us. "What happened?" An alarm went off in the house. Prabalika ran for the first-aid kit, and Rishika dialled Brijmohan's number.

"*Jijaji*, a dog has bitten Manish," shouted Rishika on the phone.

"Is it Oreo?"

"No, *jijaji*. It was some other dog that had attacked Oreo. Manish got in between to save him. Oreo will never bite Manish!"

"Was the dog vaccinated?"

"We are not sure. The owners said he is."

"But the way they and the dog behaved, I highly doubt it," Manish said from the bathroom.

As instructed, he was washing the wound with soap.

"Is Oreo fine?" Brijmohan asked.

"We will check him now."

"Take Manish to the doctor, better to get the vaccine," he instructed before disconnecting the call.

As Rishika tended to Manish, Prabalika came and scrutinised every inch of my body. Other than a slight bruise on my leg, I was fine. I might have hurt myself with a stone. Prabalika cleaned my wounds and applied Neosporin.

"Oreo, do not eat that!" Prabalika shouted in my ears, as I was trying to lick my wound to health. They do not realise I have the power to heal myself. I do not need medicines. Instead of leaving me to tend my wounds, she came and bandaged a cotton cloth on my scar so that I would not lick it anymore.

From the next day, we started avoiding the side where Tommy lived during our walks. We strolled towards the left side of our apartment. This area had a lot of shops and houses, and though there were dogs here too, none were as ferocious as Tommy. They barked at me, and I barked right back at them. We always came to a truce. Despite that, either Rishika or Prabalika would accompany us on the walk for a few days after the incident. The more the merrier for me.

Within days, the permanence of the shift became clear; no going back to the old house. I missed the garbage cans outside our streets. Thinking about them brought Blackie back in my memories. Wherever the garbage was, she could always be seen lurking around. I longed for the long walks with her, getting into those roadside pipes, our romance, eating junk off the road, and drinking blackened street water. I missed it all.

I still had my whole family, and I also had the power to let go. I started making new friends here. There were two more dogs in the vacant lot near our building. They used to stay there with the workers. They became my friends. They were timid. Initially, they barked at me, but after a couple of days, they got used to me. I would walk past their areas, and they would just stare at me. Sometimes they came near me, and we would measure each other. But other than that, they left me alone, and I did the same. I never marked their territory. I respected their authority. Don't think that I was scared, not even a bit.

Papa started taking me for walks after a few months. Manish had to travel a lot for work, so Papa took the walk duty. He was the only one who made me run. As soon as we went out of our society's main gate, he said, "Oreo, run," and with my leash in his hand, he would start running with me. We ran for miles and miles, till our breaths made it difficult to move any further. We then slowed our pace, walking and enjoying the view, sniffing the garbage (he never let me go near them though, always pulling me away) and examining another dog's poop as we walked back home. As soon as I entered the society gate, especially in the evenings, the kids playing in the society compound ran behind me. They always maintained a safe distance, never coming too close. Chanting "Oreo, Oreo, Oreo," they would walk behind me, as if rallying behind a famous personality. Maybe it was in the name, or my personality, whatever. I was the most famous dog in this apartment complex. They walked me back to my apartment, and only after I had entered my house did they leave. Few of them were brave enough to pet me, and the rest said goodbye from a distance to go back and resume their games.

I met one more of my fans here, Priyansh. Rishika was visiting us from her college during this time. She came home with a tall, dark man with long hair. He was thin as a stick and tall as a tree. I had to crane up my neck to see his face, he was *that* tall. He came inside our house, very nervous and quiet. But as soon as he saw me, he broke into a big smile. He surprised me. In my life, I've met various types of people: those who love dogs, those who avoid them, and those who hate them. But never had I ever met a dog enthusiast. Before I could do what I do best—jump on him and lick him—he cradled me in his arms and lifted me up, showering me with kisses. He was all over me, kissing and petting me.

Get off me, I wanted to yell. But he was a guest, and everyone was so happy seeing this scene unfolding. So, I endured his overt display of affection. It took him a full ten minutes before he was over the fact of meeting a dog as handsome as me. He was totally into me.

"Can I take him for a walk? *Bhaiya, please mein leke jaoon aaj Oreo ko*?" With my leash in his hand, he asked Manish.

"You will be able to control him, right?"

"Yes, *bhaiya*. I will just pull the leash."

I will just pull the leash. Come outside, I will show you.

He checked himself in the mirror display in the living room, combed his long hair back with his hands, and leashed me.

"Rishika, are you coming?"

"No, no. You both go ahead."

After quickly checking his reflection in the mirror again, we left the apartment and exited the society gate. Once out of the gate, I started pulling him towards the left. I needed a little strength to do what I had in mind. He was tall, but not strong. He got easily pulled to the left.

I could stir him in any direction. The realisation gave me wings. I started running towards the right and he ran behind me. I crossed the road amidst traffic with him trailing behind me, with my leash clenched in his hand.

"Oreo, stop."

"Oreo, wait!"

He was holding the leash, but I was the one in control. I went to the garbage bins, explored the garbage on the road, and he followed me like a devotee everywhere.

"Dirty, Oreo."

"Come out from there, Oreo."

"Oreo, no," he shouted as he stepped on to a dirty diaper laying in the garbage.

He jerked his foot to get rid of the waste stuck to his shoes. I got a whiff of the scent of a cat from the nearby apartment complex, and following it, I ran inside. Priyansh ran with me. I loved walking with him. He never objected to my authority. He gave me free rein. Who gave or took is of no consequence here. The bottom line is, I liked him. He was of use to me. Satisfied and tired, I stirred towards home.

"Hey, Priyansh! How was the walk? Were you able to control him?" asked Manish.

"Yes, *bhaiya*. He is a good boy. I could control him with his leash," Priyansh lied.

I sniggered at his lie.

"He really enjoys running, huh?"

"Yeah, he does."

"Good!"

He stayed the night with us. Next morning, Manish was getting ready to take me for my walk. He went to Priyansh and asked, "Priyansh, want to take him again?"

"No, no, *bhaiya*. You take him. You might be missing walking him."

"Priyansh, you can take him today. I always take him."

"No, *bhaiya*, please, you take him!" he pleaded.

Manish and I just smiled in response. Rishika, though, was not that understanding.

"Priyansh! We saw you and your walk with Oreo," she said, laughing.

"Oh!" He turned red.

These moments kept my family together. They believed in living life in the present and cherished every single moment.

Chapter 19

Months passed in a blur, filled with hospital visits, and Mummy's condition was deteriorating, despite everything.

Mummy continued her regular dialysis sessions, but she grew even more exhausted.

She needed a kidney transplant as soon as possible.

Talks and discussions like these started slowly dominating the conversations in my house. Lipika and Nikhil had come back; everyone was here for Mummy. A lot had changed in the family over the last few months. A few months after Priyansh's visit, Manish and Prafulla had moved away. Rishika was in Hyderabad. Prabalika, Mummy, Papa, and I were the only ones left in the house. Brijmohan used to come and go, while Lipika and Nikhil would visit for a few months each year.

This was my happiest moment as everyone was present—Nikhil, Lipika, Manish, Prabalika, Brijmohan, Prafulla, Rishika, Mummy and Papa. After 2014, this was the first time we were all together. In between Mummy's hospital visits, we went on trips.

We went on a day trip to Nandi Hills. Two Innova cars were called, one was occupied by Rishika, Lipika, Nikhil,

Papa and me, and the other with Prabalika, Brijmohan, Manish, Prafulla, and Mummy. And off we went! It was just an hour's journey, but we stopped twice for tea, once for coconut water, and once for a restroom break. We had a grand picnic on the hill. My Pedigree was there too, along with my beloved boiled eggs, water and dental sticks.

I even managed to beg for a small scoop of ice cream from them. It was a feast for me. We came back by 6:00 p.m., tired but happy. After a few days, there was a lot of commotion in the house. Bags were packed once again. First Mummy, Prabalika, and Nikhil left. Everyone cried and hugged. I still don't understand why they cry and still leave? If you don't want to go, then simply don't go. Why so much drama?

A few days later, Manish, Prafulla and Papa left too. Then the very next day, Brijmohan also left. To my disappointment, I was stuck with the two sisters: the oldest, Lipika, and the youngest, Rishika. I was worried when I realised what had happened. I was with my two least favourite people at home. The rest of the family had left in a flurry, bags in tow. It took me a while to make sense of my situation.

"Oreo! It's just us three now. Come sit in our room." I really hope everything goes fine.

"Don't worry, it will be fine. Mummy is in the hands of the best doctors," Lipika said, sitting next to me to pet me.

"Transplant is a major surgery." I could sense fear in Rishika's voice.

"It is, but Mummy will be fine. She will have a new kidney soon," Lipika consoled, trying to sound upbeat. But I could see her hiding her tears.

Then the attention was back on me again.

"*Kya kar raha hai*, Oreo?"

"Oreo, come, let's play."

You get the point now? I kid you not, 24/7 they hovered around me. I could hear my name being chanted every second, from every corner of the house. Would you like it if, from morning to night, someone kept calling your name and petting you every chance they got? No privacy. A dog needs his nap too. I had no respite, not even for a minute, from this over-the-top display of love. Every hour they came to harass me. If I moved to a different room, they would follow. If I pretended to sleep, they still sat beside me and petted me. Nothing worked with these two.

I have heard people say, "Wherever you go, your dog follows." But for me, it was the other way round. Wherever I went, these two sisters followed.

I know I am cute, and cuddly, and sweet, and all those things they say we dogs are. But hey, a guy needs his privacy. I am cute, but that doesn't mean you could be all over me *all* the time, right? I enjoy being a pet, but too much of anything is bad.

As if disturbing me was not enough, they turned their attention to the house. Yes, somehow, they got it into their heads that they were interior designers. Rishika and Lipika now planned to surprise Mummy by painting the house.

"Chhoti, let's paint the house before Mummy returns," Lipika suggested.

"Yeah, she will love it. Let's do *madhubani* designs. We can do this, right?" Chhoti added.

"Yes, we definitely can!" Lipika was always the optimist. "I will paint the walls, you do the murals. What do you think?"

They were talking as if they were professionals here. The discussion went on for hours, including deciding the paint colours and finalising the designs. The consensus was to paint an accent wall in each of the rooms, and then do the *madhubani* art over it.

"On to new beginnings!" Lipika cheered.

The very next day, the sisters got started on the task at hand. The overpowering odour of paint filled the entire house. They removed every room's furniture and piled it in the living room before they began painting. From morning to night, they just did that. Brijmohan would sometimes visit on the weekends and help them. They just kept painting and drawing designs on the walls.

I tell ya, I have never seen such subpar work. But who was I to complain? At least they left me alone while they were busy painting.

Weeks passed and finally, Lipika and Rishika were finished painting the house. They rearranged the furniture, changed the decoration, and replaced the curtains on all the windows. I have to admit though, it came together quite well. I could have done better.

I felt bored with only the three of us in the empty house. I would go sit in Mummy's room and wait for her, but no one came back.

One morning, I spotted both the sisters cooking in the kitchen for a gathering. *Pooris, sabzi,* and sweets. The entire house smelled of spices. They were making food and packing it.

Brijmohan arrived and took all the food. Was he going to eat everything? How rude! Did not even ask me for one *poori*. I don't like it, but that doesn't mean he shouldn't even ask.

Few days later, I felt immense joy to see Papa back. Seeing another man in the house made me feel happy. Taking care of these two was a major task, and I was glad someone was there to share my burden now. These two could talk non-stop for hours. It was taxing on my ears. Now I walked with Papa and found relief from their constant chatter. His return brought hope of seeing Mummy, Nikhil, and Manish again. A dog can hope, right? I kept hoping, but days became months, and they didn't come back.

One day, however, there was a lot of fanfare in the house. It surprised me to see Rishika and Lipika so happy, when just hours before they had been so silent, chanting prayers. Rishika sat in her room chanting the *Hanuman Chalisa*, while Lipika settled in the living room chanting *Mahamrityunjaya Mantra*. Papa was in his *pooja* room performing *pooja* after *pooja*. During those five hours, the only sound was the chanting. I guessed praying was for something important, so I started praying to my supreme as well. I prayed for all their prayers to be successful. After another six hours, a call came, and they all started dancing. They were crying and dancing at the same time. I joined them too. Circling around them, I moved along with them, barking and wagging my tail.

"Oreo! *Mummy ka transplant successful ho gaya*! She is fine!" Rishika rejoiced, kissing me.

I understood little of what they said, but I got that Mummy was well. Something good happened, and I was happy too. We had a party that night. I got a full scoop of ice cream.

The routine was set, and now that Papa was at home with us, I was becoming accustomed to it. But I think life doesn't want me to live in peace. It threw a curveball at me again.

I came from my evening walk one day to find the family room filled with packed bags.

Here we go again, I thought, *luggage ready once more*.

Chapter 20

Someone's moving, or maybe Mummy's back. I jumped and rushed into her room. But it was empty. Disappointed, I returned and perched on my bed, ready for whatever was to follow.

Next morning, bright and early, Papa and Lipika started moving the luggage downstairs. It included my bed too. I would get panic attacks whenever my bed was packed, because it meant I was being transported. I was used to people arriving at and departing from the house, but the thought of travelling jittered me. I watched them with apprehension as they packed my food and water bowls. They packed all my belongings, including all my toys, both my beds, and all my food.

Why can't they settle in one place and stop moving again and again? Now what is wrong with this house? I wondered. *I have friends here, the kids here are my fans, and I know the neighbourhood very well. So why are we moving again?* I kept howling, but Lipika, Rishika, and Papa continued loading the autorickshaw. Soon, Papa boarded the auto, and he pulled me in too.

Maybe we were shifting the house again and will stop soon. A dog could hope, and I did just that. I waited for the auto to stop at every building we passed. But we kept moving; we passed the trees-laden Bannerghatta Road, then the completely jammed Brigade Road, yet we still kept moving. I was beginning to feel we were going to spend the rest of our lives in the auto. Thankfully, we stopped right then. It was a railway station.

It wasn't the same place I had been to before. It was a new station. As soon as I saw it, I was happy. A train travel... I like that. We were on the move again. We unloaded and moved towards the platform. This was a cleaner, less crowded station. Apart from a few people waiting for the train, it was deserted. Deprived of humans, I mean; dogs were in abundance here. They were the rulers of this place, it seemed. Every corner and every platform had a dog roaming and guarding its territory. When we reached the platform, our train was already on the tracks, so we went inside. Although time was short, Papa still took me for a quick walk. I did what I do best: mark the territory. We were back in the cabin, and having travelled twice, I was a professional now. I jumped into my window seat and made myself comfortable. Lipika laid my treats in front of me on the white bedsheet for snacking, and I was ready for the familiar rhythmic movements of the train.

After around ten minutes, the train jerked. It started its journey, and so did we. The routine remained unchanged, getting off at every stop, regardless of it being a station or not. This train kept on stopping in the middle of nowhere. We always got down to check and mark. It was better if it was not a station, as only a few people boarded or disembarked from the train and no hawkers obstructed my view. Just a few curious souls, including me, on the tracks. Without wasting any time, I would get busy checking out the tracks and the nearby shrubs for food and traces of other dogs. As soon as we heard the train whistle, I would jump back up on the train, followed by Papa.

I enjoyed riding in the train; the movements, the thrill of getting off and jumping up, the constant sound of *chuk-chuk* made by the train's tyres, and non-stop supply of treats—everything put together made it a journey worth taking.

Early morning the next day, when I was just out of my slumber, our train stopped, and our luggage was taken out. My beds came down as well, along with my food and toys. There were two bags full of them. I had to keep track of my luggage.

"Oreo!" I jumped at the sound. It was coming from the platform. I saw him finally running towards us. Manish was here! I could not believe my eyes. My tail started wagging furiously, and my body twisted itself in joy. I started howling for Manish.

"Oreo, my boy!" He was just as happy as I was. It was pure love.

I replied with kisses and hugs. I was happy to move if it meant for Manish and me to be together. I would do anything for him.

We handed our luggage to porters and moved outside the station. I walked with the porter carrying my items. You can never be too careful. We loaded the cars and then drove home. This was again a new place. I noticed it was not Agra. The platforms were cleaner, and the people were friendlier towards me. And no one refused to take a dog in their car.

One, two, and three. I counted my bags, and both my beds were loaded in the car. Only after that I jumped into the car and took my seat.

“Welcome to Ahmedabad, Oreo,” Lipika said. She had been quiet during the entire journey.

“This is the land of Mr Modi,” Manish explained.

“You are in the land of the *chaiwala*, Oreo!” she added.

Manish’s relaxed demeanour put me at ease too.

The roads were impressively wide, but the traffic was chaotic, with vehicles darting in every direction, honking horns mingling with the distant shouts of frustrated pedestrians. Bicycles weaved through gaps in the gridlock, while motorbikes squeezed past cars that were too stubborn to move.

Drivers seemed to have their own set of rules, interpreting signals based on instinct rather than adherence to traffic laws. The traffic controller stood at the intersection, arms crossed and expression resigned, as if he had long given up on trying to impose order. His whistle was more for show than for control.

Riders zipped past without helmets, as if the thrill of the ride outweighed the need for safety. As if humans were not enough, there were cows meandering along the road in a single line. Though, in contrast to the humans, these animals seemed to embody a natural order.

The dogs, too, had their own agenda. Unlike the timid dogs I had encountered in Agra, these canines strutted with confidence, their muscles defined and their postures assertive. They seemed to own the streets, running from one corner to another, barking or engaging in the occasional tussle. As I saw two dogs locked in a fierce battle, I felt concerned—those were definitely not the kind of goons I wanted stalking my neighbourhood streets.

We reached home after twenty minutes. Prafulla was standing outside a house and that gave me the clue we were home. It was a residential neighbourhood. Few apartments and houses were standing in a semicircle. Our house was on the top floor of a two-storey building. The ground floor was the landowners' residence.

"Oreo, *chalo*," Manish said. We ran up the stairs and into the house. It was a small one. Upon entering, a converted balcony served as the living room, which had space to only hold a small single bed. It opened into a bedroom-cum-dining room. The double bed here worked both for sleeping and eating. The room opened into a kitchen and outside it, there was a tiny balcony. The stairs to the room above were inaccessible.

"*Didi*, we thought we could keep Oreo upstairs. There is a terrace attached. He will have more space there," Prafulla suggested.

"Oreo, you can stay upstairs. Want to climb?" Manish asked, pointing towards the ladder.

I tried to climb, but only managed the first step before retreating. You want to know what stairs were those? Picture two sticks standing upright and parallel to a wall, forming a ninety degree angle from it. Small planks were placed horizontally between these sticks, and each was spaced half a foot apart. This design created a staircase that was much narrower than a ladder, making it very difficult to climb.

"He is scared. I don't think he will go up," Manish guessed.

"*Ghar chota hai thoda*," Prafulla said apologetically, but I'm not entirely sure why.

"Yes, it is really small for Oreo and Papa to be comfortable," Manish added.

"The size of the house does not matter much, Manish. You remember we all stayed in a one-bedroom apartment in Bangalore. We managed then, and we can manage it now as well," Lipika reminisced.

I agreed with Lipika for once—what matters most is one's intention.

When we stepped out for a walk that evening, I was excited. New places always thrill me. They bring out the puppy in me. I loved exploring the unknown and uncharted territories. Descending the stairs from our apartment, a surprise awaited me at the gate. A gang of dogs was waiting for me. I had heard a lot of dogs barking during the day while resting at home, but this was a first. At least six dogs were waiting for me at the gate. They started barking non-stop the moment we arrived.

I dashed forward, ready to jump the gate and tackle them. I did not bark, though. When there is excessive barking, I keep quiet. I believe in conserving my energy.

"Oreo, come on," Manish said, ushering me to the apartment. I resisted. I was not one who accepted defeat without even trying.

"Oreo, *chalo*," he insisted, pulling harder at my leash. With no other choice left, I followed him back to the apartment. I walked backwards, looking at the dogs. I did not show them my back. Though Manish did.

"Manish, you are back already?" Lipika was surprised.

No, he got scared. I thought angrily.

"This area has too many dogs, and they are aggressive," Manish said, taking off his shoes.

"Maybe we all can go together so they will be scared off. There is always strength in numbers," Lipika suggested.

After ten minutes, we came out again. Papa and Lipika both kept a stick in their hands. Manish held onto my leash tightly. Those relentless dogs were still there, sitting by the tree in front of our house, waiting for me.

"Shoo, shoo!" Papa and Lipika went out first, hitting the sticks on the ground to scare them away. The dogs backed away, but only a little. Finally, we left the house. The first thing I did was mark my territory at the tree where those dogs were sitting.

It was my *tree in front of* my *house. How dare they sit there?*

I locked eyes with those dogs. Their barking erupted like a relentless storm, sharp and urgent, filling the air. I was tethered; they ran wild. Three bodyguards flanked me. They had the safety of their pack; I had the constraint of my leash. If not for the sudden tug, yanking me toward the road, the tension would have snapped into an ugly, brutal fight.

This leash—curse it—has humiliated me more times than I care to admit. I hate it particularly in moments like these, or when Blackie used to catch me leashed on my walks. I swear, in those moments, I wish I could sink into the earth and disappear beneath my own skin.

The dogs trailed us, their barks thinning yet insistent. They kept a cautious distance—likely deterred by the sticks—but shadowed us nonetheless, their eyes gleaming with primal curiosity. My bodyguards could deal with them. Anyway, it was their fault for making such a spectacle of me. If left to me, with no one holding me back, I'd have ended this chase—permanently. But everyone has a role to play. *Maybe they wanted to be heroes?* Fine. I let them do their job.

We veered toward the left side of the apartment complex, stepping onto the sidewalk along a busy road. Shops bustled around us, a mix of shouting vendors and honking cars adding to the chaos. The crowd squeezed past us, brushing shoulders and hurrying along. After five hundred metres, we turned right. The noise of the road faded behind us as we entered a quieter neighbourhood—one I knew well. Here, the buildings were sparse, giving way to an open field.

The dogs slowed and, like shadows retreating at dawn, turned back.

I watched them go, a mix of relief and amusement washing over me.

Out of their jurisdiction? Lucky me. I muttered, but my moment of peace was short-lived.

Almost instantly, barking erupted from every corner, growing louder as packs of dogs emerged from the bushes like a scene out of a wild movie. They were bold and unyielding, their confidence apparent as they surrounded us.

Papa and Lipika stood their ground, but even the sticks they wielded didn't seem enough against this unruly mob. Lipika quickly resorted to throwing small stones and dirt, to deter the aggressive canines. Papa, not one to back down, began hitting the stick against the ground, the sound resonating through the air. It was a desperate attempt to establish dominance, but these dogs had little fear of humans. They were accustomed to people's kindness and often exploited it, knowing they could intimidate anyone with their sheer numbers.

As the chaos unfolded, I could feel my heart racing, the tension in the air thickening. The dogs circled us, barking and growling, testing our resolve.

"Walk fast," Papa hissed.

"Where did so many dogs come from? They seem to be rabid," Lipika whispered.

"Yeah, people here treat them kindly, and no one hurts them, so they are not scared of us," Manish said urgently.

"That is good. People should do that everywhere," Lipika remarked, clearly impressed before adding, "but we need to get out of here and find another area for Oreo."

We quickened our pace, hurrying across the field to reach the gated community and escape the aggressive mutts. Dogs prioritise their own territories and have clearly defined boundaries they don't cross. Sure enough, they stopped at the perimeter, content as long as we stayed out of their area.

But even though I exited their field, I wasn't about to let it slide. I knew exactly how to get back at them. I did what I do best and what I knew would annoy them the most—I marked the edges of their field just before dashing into the society complex.

Payback time, boys. I looked back at them and gave a smug smile as I entered the gate.

Inside, the atmosphere shifted to one of calm and order. I noticed a couple of well-behaved dogs, all leashed and strolling with their human family, just like me. They seemed to embody the calmness of the community, a complete contrast to the wild chaos outside.

We wandered around the complex, the neatly manicured lawns and peaceful pathways offering us a respite from the earlier tension. But maybe I spoke of it a little too soon. A persistent cooing caught my attention. At first it was very feeble, but then its intensity grew. I looked at Manish, but he was busy talking with Lipika and Papa. I tried nudging him towards the sound; when that did not work, I pulled the leash hard in the direction of the cry.

"Oreo! Stop!" Manish said, untangling himself from the leash.

"You made me fall," he said, now getting up.

That is what happens when you are not attentive. I thought and waited for him to be stable.

"Oh! Lipika, do you hear some bird cooing painfully nearby? Can you?" Manish questioned as he walked in that direction.

Finally, they got it. I sighed and followed him quickly.

"Oh no!" Manish gasped, quickly bending down to pick up the source of the sound—an injured sparrow.

"She is badly hurt but is still breathing."

"Looks like she fell from that tree," Lipika said.

"We need to take her to a vet, otherwise she might not survive." Manish was determined.

"We will take Oreo home. You take her to the vet," Papa said.

"Thank you, Oreo. You helped rescue a bird today," Lipika said, petting me tenderly.

We made our way back home, the excitement of the day still burning in my veins, but tempered by the familiar comfort of safety.

The next morning, once again, Manish, Papa, and Lipika accompanied me. But this time, instead of left, we took a right from our apartment. This zone buzzed with unusual activity. People in tracks zoomed past us, running with headphones in their ears. Besides people jogging or practising yoga, there was minimal traffic on this road. And no dogs. We walked for about a kilometre in peace, enjoying the silence for once and that's when I heard clapping.

Hmm, I think the people knew who was visiting—me, the great Oreo! Wow! So, just like Bangalore, I had a fan club here too. People worship me, and rightly so if you ask me!

I was busy appreciating myself when I heard a roar of laughter from the same group. A forced and fake laughter.

"Look, a laughter club," Lipika said.

People stood in a circle, clapping and laughing in frenzy. I mean, there was no joke being told, no prank being played, and still these people clapped and laughed. Man, humans act crazy sometimes.

Apart from the human craziness, our walk remained uneventful. From now on, this would be our regular path for walks.

Life again settled back into a routine. Lipika left a few days later. Papa, Manish, Prafulla and I remained in the house. Mummy was still not here. I could see her on video calls, but she was still in the old Bangalore house.

She seemed better and better on each call, which made me very happy. Both Manish and Prafulla left for work in the mornings and returned in the evening. Papa and I stayed at home. He would take me for walks in the evenings after his *pooja*. Manish took me for walks in the mornings. Sometimes even Prafulla accompanied us; our relationship had become cordial. Neither I would trouble her, nor would she trouble me. When she came from the office, I just wagged my tail from a distance, and she greeted me. She did not pet me much, and I never approached her bed again.

Chapter 21

On the first anniversary of my move to Ahmedabad, I reflected back on the year and everything that had happened. The dogs in my neighbourhood got used to my presence and accepted me. By accepting, I do not mean they started loving me or welcoming me, they simply tolerated me. They still barked whenever I took walks in the mornings and evenings, but they no longer followed me, having realised I wasn't a threat to them.

I made another record this year, but I'm not proud of it; with regret and shame, I acknowledge that I had failed to escape the house even once this entire time. It's not that I did not try. I did, but there were so many hurdles! Manish's house was on the first floor. This one was built on a higher ground, unlike the one in Bangalore. Oh boy! How I used to run out of our Bangalore apartment, almost every month! Even though we lived in a gated community, I used to manage running out. That was one of the main reasons for my fame. I stood out as the only dog from my building complex who received recognition from the security guards. And not just every watchman, but also every nearby shop owner knew me well. Fame and name require taking risks. No risk, no fame. The other dogs in my building had no fan following, no kids walked behind them chanting their names, and none of the security guards ever said hi to them. They lived in oblivion. Unlike them, I had a very active social life, that included running away from the house.

Well, what to do? I *am* that exceptional.

You want to know how to do it? I will share my secrets with you all. I am quite generous too.

So, let's go back to my Bangalore story: my bed was placed in the living room, right next to the balcony that offered me a direct view of the front door. I would watch it like a hawk for any movement. The first rule to successfully running away from home is that you have to be perseverant; watching the door once or twice in a day will not do. You must be vigilant at all times. If someone rang the doorbell, I opened my eyes and watched. If it was a delivery, I waited for them to leave the door ajar, and off I ran. The second thumb rule: act fast if you find an opening. No second-guessing, and no waiting for the right moment. You notice the door open, you sprint towards it. Got it? Also, not just for the doorbell, if I heard any movement or a slight click, I would be on alert. In such situations, I would stand behind the door and wait for it to open. It is difficult, yes, but I am telling you, if you plan and keep trying, there will always be a way out.

The best time to run out was during the online deliveries. In the hurry to get packages inside, my family would often leave the door ajar, and never one to miss a chance, I would dash out. Bangalore's new apartment's design encompassed only one level, presenting both advantages and disadvantages. The merit was that I could see everyone and be with my family at the same time. I no longer needed to climb stairs to meet them. But this became a major setback as well, because they'd notice my absence as soon as I left. I would seldom get a good head start, unlike my first house, where by the time they searched and realised I was not upstairs, I would get a good ten-fifteen minutes on them.

At the Ahmedabad apartment, my family would start making calls to the security guards as soon as I am on my way down the stairs. Unfortunately, regardless of my speed, by the time I would arrive at the society's entrance, the guards would be closing the gates. Yes, the phones worked faster than my legs.

Dejected, but not disheartened, I would use whatever little time I would get to explore my apartment complex. Even within the society, I would make my family run behind me for at least twenty minutes before relenting and getting caught. Thumb rule three: no matter what the hardships are, try to make the best of it. Even with society gates closing before I could get out, and everyone acting against me, I never stopped trying. Remember, persistence always pays. I used a new strategy and ran faster than the speed of sound, outsmarting the phone. By the time the security guard would get off the phone with my family, I would be out of the front gate. Sometimes, I'd manage to run out just as the gate was closing. Glancing at the guards, I would twist my head and sprint in any direction that caught my interest.

It would be me and my freedom, though not for long; my family had learnt persistence from the best—me. Within ten minutes, I would hear my name being called. I would turn back, look and smile at them, and then run off at double the speed. Cursing, they would also run faster. It was a fun game of cat and mouse. Only in this game, it was the mouse who always decided when to be caught.

On one such adventure outside my house, I took a right from my building, and immediately turned left. I was under the influence of an intoxicating smell. It was coming from straight ahead, so I increased my pace. I came to a halt in a marketplace, and it was nothing short of heaven. There was a strong smell of fish everywhere. The smell of drying, fresh, rotten, and dried fishes came together and created an unparalleled aroma. It was nothing like I had ever smelled before. It was my lucky day; I even found a small piece of fish lying on the ground near the trash can. Before anyone could stop me, I picked it up in my mouth and gulped it. It was pure bliss! I would have loved to explore the area more, enjoying more such morsels, but time was running out. My family was on my heels, so I ran from there, reluctantly moving my paws away from this heaven.

I ran for another ten minutes, stopping in between to explore the locality. It was some time before I heard my name. Worried, I looked back. Yeah, I had to check back on them periodically to see if they were coming behind me or not. What if they get lost and go the wrong way? I am responsible for them, you know. So, when I looked back, I saw their backs to me. They were walking backwards. Confused, I stood and watched them. The distance between us was increasing. That is when I realised, they were not walking backwards, they were going in the wrong direction. They were headed back to the house!

How dare they leave me?

I could not bear the thought. I ran behind them, knowing well that I was walking into a trap. The things we do for family, I tell ya. But I digress; the point I am trying to make is that I am a professional at running away from the house, but to my disappointment and despite my persistence in the Ahmedabad house, I never got the chance. It wasn't that my family got smarter than me. No, that is impossible. The issue here was with the engineering of the front doors. You see, there were two types of doors here: the usual wooden door and a self-closing metal mesh door. Notice the irony: the entrance of this house was always open so that I could glimpse the outside world, breathe in the freedom, but always needed a human companion to open the self-closing door. It closed on its own within a second of being open unless someone held it open. I am fast, but I am not stupid. As soon as anyone came or left, this door would close even before they had exited fully. I couldn't outrun it. I hate such feats of the mighty engineers. I hate them altogether. Period. I know I have two of them in my family. But I still hate engineers and their automatic doors.

Apart from that, life was normal, except for the daily reminder of my diminishing power to flee. I spent most of my time at home with Papa. Prafulla and Manish went to the office. Sometimes Papa and Manish took me for walks, and other times a dog walker came to take me out.

Now let me enlighten you on the breed of dog walkers. To all my fellow beings, if you are offered a chance to have a stranger walk you, please take it up. I know it sounds weird to be escorted on your walks by a total stranger while your own family is busy sleeping or working. But trust me, it's quite advantageous. Firstly, the dog walkers never make you walk more than you want to. Like in my case, whenever Papa took me for walks, he made me run for miles in the name of exercise. That was tiring, man. But with the walkers, we would hardly complete the mile-long walk around the neighbourhood. My walker would then sit with his friends, other walkers, and have long discussions. Second, they are not cleanliness freaks. See, when I went for a walk with anyone from the family, they never let me go near the garbage, always immediately pulling me back. But with dog walkers, they never stop you. I had the fortune of exploring all the dustbins in my area on my walks with the walker. He even allowed me the luxury to go to the huge garbage dumps by the side of the road. Exploring all the corners of this dump, filled with smells of all kinds, was a treat for my senses. I sometimes even got a hold of a half-eaten chicken stick or a leftover fish. I looked forward to these walks. The thought of treasures I would find on my walks kept me awake at night. If you are health-conscious, this might not interest you; you might even object to less exercise as well, but I am a contented soul. I am happy with whatever I have. As for exercise, I always keep my weight at twenty-four kilograms and no more. I've never exceeded that weight in my life.

On the days when I found special treats in the dump yards, I would portion-control my dinner. I'd eat less. This is how you manage your weight. No major science here. If you eat extra once, just eat less during the next meal. Enjoy life, I'd say, with your dog walkers. They are a rare breed.

My equation with Prafulla at home was positive now. We both loved Manish, and our mutual love for him made us compatible with each other. Most of the time she kept to herself, but on days Manish was late from work, she'd feed me. One day, I remember precisely as she cried after feeding me. Manish was late as usual. She came with my bowl at sharp 7:00 p.m. and gave me my usual food of rice, chicken, and eggs. We do not cook chicken. My family is puritan. But they'd get packets of chicken meat for me. I would eat the chicken with utmost sincerity, not spilling it anywhere, and would finish my meal in time too. I knew it was a big sacrifice for my family, letting me have chicken, and I respected them for it.

When she started crying, I wondered if I should have saved some for her. Was she hungry? I was feeling guilty. Thankfully, Papa came out of the *pooja* room right then and saw her crying. "What happened, *beta*?" he inquired.

"*Papa, meine aaj chicken ko hath lagaya*. This is the first time I have had to touch it. I have already washed my hands more than ten times, yet I still feel dirty."

"Sorry, *beta*. From tomorrow, give him only vegetarian meals," Papa replied.

I am okay eating curd and rice, Prafulla. Please don't cry because of me. I howled and tried to calm her. I was touched that she went to such lengths for me. She could not see me hungry, and though it was against her beliefs, she fed me chicken.

She had come around and had fallen in love with me after all, I realised.

She even bathed me once. Don't get me started on my baths, man. It is the one thing I hate the most in this world. I hate water, except for when I drink it. I want nothing to do with it. Humans like taking a bath, I get it. They shower daily; I see my family members voluntarily going into the bathrooms with towels on their shoulders and singing to themselves. They are brave in this regard, I must admit, readily enduring such discomfort. But for me, even my monthly baths are a torture.

"Oreo, *chalo nahane*." Hearing this every month is a death sentence to me. As soon as I hear anyone calling me for baths, I would try my best to hide. Sometimes I hide under the bed, other times I would curl up into a ball in my bed, hoping for them to not see me. I would even try wagging my tail and rolling beside them to bribe them. I tried eating my food on my own and behaving like a true gentleman, thinking that would save me from this torture, but it was to no avail. Once every month in winters, and every fifteen days in summers, I had to endure this torture my family called a bath.

If you saw it from the outside, I resembled a ceremonial sacrifice, ready to be butchered. They would pull me with my leash, and I would pull hard in the other direction to avoid going to the bathroom. I used all my strengths at such times, but these people, my own family, would be relentless. They'd keep saying nice things, yet continue doing the opposite.

"Oreo, my dear boy," Lipika used to say while pulling me hard.

"Bath time, good boy." Instead of giving me treats for being good, Manish would drag me to the bathroom.

"You'll be clean after the bath," Prafulla would shout, but I never complained that I was dirty.

They'd kept up this chatter the whole time to get me into the bathroom, as if I was a fool. I understood everything. They just wanted to waste water. And if taking a bath was not enough of a hardship, I had to endure their additional love after the bath, too, especially if the sisters were around.

"Wow, Oreo, you're so soft now."

"Let me touch your hair, Oreo, it's so silky!"

They'd even call everyone in the house, or anyone visiting at that time, and ask them to pet me.

"*Jijaji, isko chuiye*. See, how soft he is."

"Hey, check Oreo, he looks so cute. He's taken a bath today."

And those baths weren't the end of it. In between, they'd also take me to spas, where they'd have my nails cut, ears cleaned, and teeth brushed. I failed to understand why they put themselves through similar torture daily! As I said, humans can really be crazy sometimes.

The only thing I liked about a bath was the food that was served to me afterwards. Additional treats would be laid out on my clean bed (even my bedsheets would get a bath the day I got one) with a bowl full of milk, ready to be licked dry.

These people, my own family members, would happily participate in my torturous ritualistic bath; Lipika, Rishika, and Prabalika felt that my bathing was the most important thing in the world, so they would be hovering over me during my baths; Manish and Nikhil were also happily involved, much to my dismay. And now, Prafulla joined them too. She gave me a bath in Ahmedabad, and she started acting weird after that. She would stare at me. I mean literally stare into my eyes.

Worry filled my mind as I repeatedly checked for eye irritations, acne, and signs of grey hair on my face. But nothing was wrong with me. I was clueless. Before going to work and after coming back, she would hunch down to stare at me. She'd even smile while looking in my eyes. She'd never say a word. She'd just *look*. To be honest with you, it totally freaked me out the day I noticed Manish doing the same thing!

Am I getting old? What is the issue? Do I have a terrible disease? Have I done something bad? Is it bath time again?

I went mad with these thoughts running through my mind. And then one day, I heard her talking to my sisters.

"Lipika *didi*, I have read that if you look into a dog's eyes, unblinking, they feel loved."

"Just look?"

"Yes, just look into their eyes. I've started doing it with Oreo. Manish is doing it too."

"Great! We will do it too. He will feel loved."

Are these guys insane? Well, after listening to this conversation, I felt relieved that I was not the one who was crazy here.

Staring into my eyes will give me the feeling of being loved? I still can't believe they'd listen to such bizarre advice by the so-called experts in newspapers and magazines. *Instead of staring, how about giving me more treats?* Can someone please suggest this to the writer of this useless information? I am still trying to dig out the source of that information.

Humans and their craziness; it never ends, does it?

Life would have continued in the same way, but a knock on our door one day changed everything again.

On hearing the knock, I inched forward towards the door, expecting the mailman or a delivery guy. No one else came here. It was not like the Bangalore house, where so many of my family members kept visiting. Even Rishika, who was a regular in Bangalore, would hardly visit. So, I was surprised to see Lipika standing behind that metal door.

That didn't make me exceptionally elated, but she was family. Finally, after a whole year, she was visiting me. In short, I was happy. I welcomed her with my tail wags and licked her face. At last, someone from my family, other than the ones I was living with, remembered me. But her visits were now overshadowed by a sense of lingering doom; whenever she came, she brought some or the other change for me. I have put two and two together and now I know: whenever she visited, my bags would be packed, and I would move. First it happened when I had to visit Agra, then back to Bangalore, next to another house in Bangalore, and then to Ahmedabad, and here she was again. Was I going to travel again?

So, I guess now you can understand why I greeted her with mixed emotions. Even though I was happy, a whimper or two escaped my mouth.

"Oreo, *kya hua*?" Lipika asked me as I sat on my bed, deep in thought, preparing myself for my next journey.

I knew travel was inevitable now, and sure enough, a few days later my fears came true. Lipika was in Ahmedabad for only ten days, during which new suitcases were bought and, soon enough, packed with tons of stuff. I got a new crate too. It was huge, like a small room. I enjoyed sitting in it because it somehow comforted me.

"He likes his crate!" Manish beamed like a happy parent.

A lot of trips to the vet followed. Then Lipika left, leaving all the packed bags and my bed behind. I took a sigh of relief. I was not travelling this time. I thought I was safe, but I couldn't have been more wrong.

Chapter 22

While coming back from my walk one evening, a couple of days after Lipika left, I noticed a huge SUV parked right under the tree in front of our home.

Someone was visiting! I ran and wagged my tail excitedly. I was halfway up the stairs, with my dog walker running behind me, when I saw Prafulla coming down with a bag.

Oh no, someone was leaving. I barked at her once to greet her and raced up, entering the living hall howling. *It shouldn't be Manish,* I kept praying.

"Oreo! *Chalo...* We are going to Mumbai," Manish announced, coming out of the kitchen with my food bowl.

In the meantime, the SUV was packed again, with the bags and enormous suitcases that Lipika had packed. They moved my crate to the car, ignoring my protests. Once I finished eating, I was told to hop into the SUV. I kept howling until I saw Papa and Manish get into the car with me. I relaxed then.

Prafulla petted me, said goodbye, and then we departed. As we navigated through the afternoon traffic in Ahmedabad, I relaxed on my mat and dozed off. I knew it would be a long drive, so I made myself comfortable. Ordinarily, I liked auto rides more than cars, as autos were open on two sides, but the SUV ride wasn't too bad. After crossing the city limits, the roads cleared of traffic and got wider. Our car was touching a hundred by then. With windows open, I was basking in the cool night air. This was not bad at all. A few hours later, we stopped at a roadside stall for tea. I took a walk on the moonlit night, a soft breeze blowing on my face and the trees swaying as if to welcome me. The only thing missing was my beloved Blackie.

"Oreo, come back in the car."

And with that, we were back on the road again. The same cycle continued for the rest of the night. We stopped every few hours for tea and a stroll. Papa does not drink tea, so he just walked with me. In the wee hours of the morning, we entered Mumbai.

"Oreo, welcome to the city of dreams. It's the home of Bollywood, where all movies are made," Manish explained.

The last statement made me sit up and take notice. I wanted to be an actor too. It was my childhood dream. Through my experiences of watching countless TV soap operas with Mummy and tons of movies with Manish and Brijmohan, I felt I was ready too. If you ask me, acting is not that difficult. Don't we all act in our real lives too all the time?

Remember the last time you acted? When your friend asked you out, and you didn't want to go. What did you do? Say no on their face or act and give an excuse? Think back to the time you manipulated your parents to get a toy by crying, throwing tantrums, and yelling until you had the toy. We all act. But only a few of us are smart enough to earn money from it. I wanted to be one of them. I had watched many dog-centric movies, and I knew I could act better than those canine actors, if only I were given a chance.

Maybe *this* was my chance. I will try! I charged up with new enthusiasm and started looking around fully alert. Every city I've been to since my youth has been distinct, not just in infrastructure but also in culture and people's conduct. The roads in Mumbai seemed to be similar to Ahmedabad and Bangalore. Mumbai roads were filled with cars too; the only difference was that they hardly moved. The traffic jam was worse than I had ever witnessed. It took us five hours to cover just ten kilometres. Yes, five hours! And, man, the place was jammed not only with cars, but with people as well.

Everyone was here in the city, famous for converting dreams to reality, with aspirations in their pocket and stars in their eyes. We inched forward at the speed of a snail. Bored, I just observed people on the roads and in the cars. Everyone was in a rush. People bumped into each other hurriedly. They were looking at the ground or walking at the speed of a jet. Yeah, people moved faster than cars here. Everyone was walking on the sidewalks. They resembled zombies, not even aware of where they were going or what place they were at. Few of them just let the crowd nudge them forward. The sidewalk was by the side of the sea. The famous Arabian Sea, I reckon. It was dark blue waters stretching for miles and miles. I have to admit, I was not happy to see so much water. You all know my equation with water. Thinking about what would happen if I were to be given a bath there gave me shudders. The water seemed endless, and I suppose the bath would be too. How terrifying!

"Oreo, *dekho* ocean." Manish said with childlike excitement.

"*Kitna sundar hain na*? So peaceful and serene..." Papa added thoughtfully.

I sat back on my bed, not interested in their talks anymore. I, for the life of me, couldn't understand how water could be calming for anyone. It was for Manish, I guess. He takes showers two times a day, and boy, don't even get me started on Papa. If given a chance he would happily take a bath four-five times a day, maybe more.

For many, the sea is peaceful, but for me, it's turbulent.

After sailing through the traffic for five hours, our car finally picked up the pace. It was nearly ten in the morning, and I was hungry.

"Let's stop here for fifteen minutes," Manish told the driver, and we parked near the road. I had been eagerly waiting for this. As soon as Papa opened the door, I ran out and stretched. I could see the sea by my side now. I'm fine as long as I'm far away from it, and the water doesn't touch me. The inviting and soothing coolness of the sea breeze put me at ease and made me feel welcomed. A quick walk later, we were back on the road again. I had my dry food, then nestled for a nap again.

The first stop we made was at a government building. Well, at least it looked like one. How could I tell? From its old, tattered exterior and the prominent betel nut spit marks on the walls. Undeniably a government building. These marks are a trademark of almost all the public buildings in our country. I think humans take pride in it.

Pure white walls, dirtied with red marks, especially near the midsection of the wall—it seems like an art form in itself, created by the country's betel nut eaters.

"Oreo, come," Manish called, opening the car.

He took me and my medical documents inside the building.

"We have come here for your clearance certificate," he explained.

We were in and out of the building within fifteen minutes.

The car was moving at a normal speed now, and we stopped in front of an apartment building. The place we got down at was in a less crowded neighbourhood of Mumbai, filled with trees and surrounded by under-construction buildings. A guard was present at the entrance gate, but unlike Bangalore, no yellow wall was visible. The guard helped Papa and Manish take the luggage to our apartment. It was almost two in the afternoon when I boarded the lift and reached the eleventh floor. Lipika was standing outside the door, carrying the luggage inside.

Of course! I thought, seeing her there. I should have guessed: if I was moving, she had to be around.

"Oreo, my boy," she hugged me.

With a fake grin plastered on my face, I wagged my tail half-heartedly for a few seconds before stepping in. It was a one-bedroom apartment with a tiny kitchen. While my family got busy with moving the rest of the stuff inside and unpacking and repacking the previously packed bags, I relaxed on my bed, placed near the living room sofa. My family is crazy, as you might know by now. So, I left them all to their own devices.

By five in the evening, I ventured out for my first-ever walk in the city of dreams. *I have to be at my best behaviour,* I reminded myself. You never know when and where a director might watch you. I'd read a lot of rags-to-riches stories of people in Mumbai.

We stepped out of our apartment. Manish and Lipika walked alongside me. Papa was busy with his *pooja*.

"*Kya hua,* Oreo, you don't like Mumbai?" Lipika asked. She was an excellent observer; I have to give her that. She noticed my change in behaviour instantly.

"You are right. He is not even running to the garbage bins," Manish chimed in.

"I think we should settle in Mumbai. What do you think, Oreo?"

"*Maan gaye*. Mumbai changed Oreo in just one day. Wah!"

Little did they know about my actual motive for behaving properly. I wanted to appear like a highly trained dog. Smells of fish beckoned me, and I could even see a chicken bone sticking out of a garbage can. But no, I told myself. I diverted my attention by observing the dogs in this neighbourhood. It was easy to forget about them in Mumbai unless you were looking for them; they were practically invisible here.

The dogs in the area can tell you a lot about the place. In Mumbai, the dogs were quieter and minded their own business. They were not concerned much about new dogs in their territory. They were not easily threatened either as they did not bark at me or try to chase me away.

Even when I started marking in their territory, which, by the way, I did in the most gentlemanly manner possible—slight tilt of the head to show my confidence, rear leg lifted at exactly sixty-five degrees, no more, no less, and aiming straight at the target—still they did not bother. Once I left, they re-marked the areas again. That is the best use of the non-violence policy I have ever seen in my life. If I marked it again, they would wait for me to leave and would re-mark it once again. Wow! I left the place with a new admiration for Mumbai dogs. Even though I tried to be my best self, no one with a camera or wearing a director's cap approached me. Besides that, the walk was delightful. The roads were cleaner, the people didn't bother about the stray dogs, and they didn't care about the other dogs. We returned home after an hour. Manish got boiled eggs for me from a nearby stall. After having a filling meal, I went to my bed, leaving my humans to do what they loved the most—packing.

The next morning, we went for a walk again but this time along the seaside. The early morning sea view was stunning. Surprisingly, there were hardly any people. Apart from a few runners, we had the beach all to ourselves. Rare, given the amount of people I've seen in Mumbai thus far. I was still on my best behaviour, but not for long. I saw a brown creature walking towards the rocks. It had several legs, and its body was shiny brown. I had to get near, see it closely and play with it. He looked like my yellow Kong toy but with legs. I rushed forward and pulled Lipika with me.

"Oreo, wait... Ouch!" She cried.

I turned back to see Lipika lying in the mud face down. Serves her right for not having kept up with me. She appeared to be in pain, so I rushed towards her, leaving the toy for later. Manish came running from the other side as well. It was just a minor injury; she was being unnecessarily dramatic. After letting her rest for a respectable five minutes, I tried running towards that creature again.

"He wants to go to that side," she said and handed the leash to Manish.

"*Chal*, Oreo," Manish said, and we ran to the creature to see him crawl under the rock.

Manish laughed heartily. "It's a crab, Oreo. An orange crab!"

Orange? His eye checkup is way overdue!

I dug into the sand near the rock to catch him. First, I tried with one leg, trying to be sophisticated, but the sand barely shifted. *To hell with the movie role*, I decided, and dug with all my might using both my front legs. I eventually saw the little creature sitting under the rock, crawling further inside, trying to avoid the sand I was throwing. I watched him go further inside, beyond my reach. So, I let it be, and we returned home. My toys were better than the crab.

We went for a stroll at dusk, too, and right when I began to get comfortable with my new routine and started thinking of Mumbai as my new home, I saw an SUV standing in front of our building and our luggage being loaded in it. I think I needed to stop thinking that things were definite. My family loaded my crate, and I settled into it.

To be honest, I was now getting used to this nomadic lifestyle; travelling freely and spending a few days in one place before moving on to the next one. It wasn't so bad. It was freeing in a way. No forming attachments to places—simply visit, enjoy, observe, and then move on. A true globetrotter. After navigating our way through the heavy Mumbai traffic, our taxi stopped outside a vast building. The outside area was filled with taxis and people. I could hear the planes landing and taking off in the vicinity. As I exited the taxi, a plane flew directly overhead, causing me to duck. We then saw a few more of such planes before we could reach the entrance.

"Oreo, get inside the crate. You cannot walk inside the airport," Lipika pushed me into the crate, and Manish petted me while I was getting in. His voice was breaking, and tears filled his eyes. *I don't mind the crate so much*, I tried telling him. I licked his hand as he closed my crate, and then off we went inside the airport.

I was impressed with the lighting; it was like Diwali inside. Every corner glowed with a thousand-watts bulbs. The place was buzzing with people moving around with suitcases and babies in tow. I saw different types of people—young, old, male, female—except for dogs. I didn't see any dogs here, not even one. Perhaps that's why I had to stay in the crate. Dogs weren't allowed here. That could be why Manish was sad. He loves me, but he also loves dogs in general. He feeds stray dogs every night, either my leftover food or bread and biscuits.

I settled in my crate, seeing no chance of getting out. That is when I saw that along with my toys, Manish had also packed his shirt in my crate. I was furious! They spent so much time packing, unpacking, and carrying such enormous suitcases, yet he had no place to keep his shirt? This was not done! If he was travelling, why did he not pack his own bag? There was surely no need to use my crate for his stuff. I don't like clutter, and Manish knew that.

I sat on top of his shirt to crumple it further than it already was. I decided to teach him a lesson he would never forget. I snuggled my face in the collar of his shirt and nestled in for a sleep. Ignoring the breach of my privacy, I enjoyed sniffing his smell in my crate. It felt as if he was sitting beside me.

Chapter 23

The airport was bustling with life. You won't think it was past midnight. We joined a queue, and Lipika moved forward with the documents to the counter. There was some discussion. She returned, collected additional documents, and went back again. After a while Manish joined her too. They both came back dejected.

"France Airlines is saying we'd need a Schengen visa to take Oreo."

"But why? We won't be exiting the aircraft," Papa said.

"Yes, but if we are taking a pet, it's different. We will have to collect him from the luggage section, feed him, and then they will reload him onto the connecting flight. And to access the luggage section, we'll need the visa," Lipika explained.

"Did they not inform you about it?" Manish asked, stunned.

"No. Give me a minute. Let me call Nikhil," Lipika said, fumbling for the phone.

She spoke to Nikhil, and then placed some more calls and had further discussions.

Defeated, Lipika said, "There's no way around. We will need a visa. What should we do now? We cannot take Oreo without a Schengen visa."

"Should we cancel the flight?" Papa asked.

"I can't. I have to join the office in three days."

"But we won't get a Schengen visa in three days... Maybe you and Papa should go?" Manish suggested thoughtfully. "I will take Oreo back to Ahmedabad, and we'll figure it out later." He reassured Lipika.

"But you and Prafulla have offices too, and Oreo hates staying alone," Papa was also worried about me.

"Let me check with Rishika. Maybe she can help," Lipika said hopefully.

Hours of discussion later, during which I'd dozed off, I jolted up because of some movement. Lipika was hovering over my crate, teary-eyed. She said goodbye, and she and Papa left through a gate beside the counter. I howled after them, but Manish quietly watched as they disappeared into the crowd. Then he took my crate, and we exited the airport once more.

Seated in a taxi, Manish and I were on our way again by 4:00 a.m. He slept off the moment we sat in the cab. I snuggled closer to him in the back seat and dozed too. We stopped just once on the journey back, and that too only for me to relieve myself. Manish didn't even have tea. He was lost in his thoughts.

After ten in the morning, I could see familiar surroundings. We were back in Ahmedabad. Why did we embark on this needless journey if we had to return? My family has a knack for wasting time and money. Prafulla was waiting for us at home, ready to leave for office. My food was ready—a bowl of curd and rice—and Manish fed me first before going and having his tea. For him, I am always his priority.

I was tired after this journey. Twenty-four hours of road journey within three days takes a toll on you, no matter how strong, young, and resilient you are. I slept right off, only to wake up late in the evening when my walker came knocking, eager to take me on my walk.

I was so drained, I didn't notice Manish and Prafulla's absence until later that day. But the following day, when they left for work, I became agitated. Why did they leave me alone? What did I do wrong now? Why couldn't one of them stay with me? Was it too much to ask for a 24/7 companion? Why was it so difficult for people to understand that a dog needs companionship 24/7? I *had* to get their attention back on me.

I started pacing the house, howling non-stop. I looked under the bed, just in case they felt like playing hide-and-seek with me. Today, I ventured into the forbidden area—the pantry, to search for them. No one was there. I looked outside from the back balcony and saw it was mostly empty, aside from a few people walking by. I stood there and called out to them. Maybe these people could lead me to my family. I was tired, but no one came forward to help. People would look up, notice me, and then leave. No words of sympathy, and no one to tell me the whereabouts of my family. I got nothing out of them. I kept howling to call out to Manish. No sign of him even though it was almost afternoon. I was hungry, and I saw my bowl filled with food, but I couldn't eat. Whenever I was tense, I'd fast for my family's safety. It was 2:00 p.m. when I heard Manish's bike and moments later, he came rushing in.

"Oreo, why are you crying so much? I got a complaint from our landowner. If you continue this, we will have to leave the house."

He was petting and scolding me at the same time. I howled in response. He must know by now I disliked solitude. He should not leave me alone at home if he was so worried about the complaints of my howling.

He fed me, and then he stayed at home with me. Prafulla came in the evening and my family was complete. I felt content. I left them both alone and went to enjoy my walk with the walker. I can leave them alone, but they should not do that to me. That was the rule back then, and it is even now. Returning from my walk, I noticed two new suitcases near the door in the living room. *I hope Lipika is not back.* I rushed in to see Rishika sipping tea sitting on the sofa.

"Oreo! My boy."

One devil was gone, so another came to visit me, I thought as I wagged my tail in mock happiness.

"*Mera chotu-motu kaisa hain?*"

Motu? I am not *motu*. I have an admirably well-chiselled body, like that of a stallion. Scolding, I howled at her. But she didn't quite get the point, and kept on calling me *motu*.

Next morning was business as usual. Manish took me for a walk and fed me. After that he and Prafulla left for the office. I was left with Rishika. Thankfully, she sat on the balcony engrossed in a book, leaving me alone. I went to sleep in the room, cuddled on my bed. I was no longer worried. She was family, after all. No matter how much she got in my face, she was still family.

You might get the notion I am being hateful towards her. I admit I do, but not without my reasons. Rishika had hit me once, and she hit me really hard. The story goes back a few years, when we were in BTM Layout house, and I was off on my daily pursuit of happiness with Blackie. That day, Rishika was chasing me, yelling my name. Hurriedly, in order to escape her, I crossed the lane and entered a restricted area. It was the territory of mafia dogs. They were brutal. Wanting to avoid one trouble, I landed myself in another. As if waiting for me, five gigantic dogs surrounded me. I was tiny then, and they started closing in on me. I heard a loud thump of a stick and saw Rishika standing in front of the dogs. She wrapped me in her arms, picked me up, and brought me home. All was fine until then, and I was just about to thank her for saving my life. But as soon as we were inside the house, she hit me.

"You could have died, you stupid dog. Why do you have to run away? Are we not enough for you? No one stops you from spending hours on the terrace. So, what is your problem, honestly?" She was talking and hitting me.

She hit me twice on my nose, and I could never forget it. As for her questions, I prefer not to answer them. That is my choice. I do not think she will ever understand freedom. She never hit me again, not out of love, but because I had grown up, and she was scared. I was hit by Manish and Nikhil, too, for the same reason (I'm unsure why they disliked me going away so much). I never hit them when they went out. In fact, I always welcomed them back with my hugs and kisses. Humans are weird, if you ask me.

We had a good time this time though. Rishika never bothered me, and in return I didn't bother her. She spent the day reading, and I spent my time sleeping. As long as I was not alone, I was at my best behaviour.

Few weeks went by, and Rishika went back. I was a little worried about being left alone and started practising my howls. The morning after she left, as Manish and

Prafulla got ready for work, I prepared for a miserable day.

"Oreo, let's go." It took me a few seconds to respond to Manish's command. It was quite unexpected. I had my walk, and Manish was ready with his bag in his hand. Why is he asking me to go with him? Has he gotten me a job at his office? Would I now need to work? Earn my keep? Thoughts like this plagued my mind. It was still a better option than being left alone. I got up from my bed, stretched my body, and followed him out of the house. We boarded an auto that was parked outside our building. It was a long ride; we crossed the residential areas of Ahmedabad and moved towards the outskirts of the city. Surrounded by natural beauty, the area was filled with lush greenery and towering trees. Our auto entered a narrow side lane, and we traversed through the trees towards a huge bungalow. *Wow! Manish works at a luxurious location*, was my first thought. We stopped at a single-storeyed building, painted with a mix of brown and white colours, looking elegant. Open area surrounded the building on all the sides, and it had about an acre of open space. Getting closer to the building, I saw a pool on the left. Not a swimming pool, but more like a man-made mud puddle. Dog toys were scattered everywhere on the lawn. And then I saw them—dogs. They were lying in the pool, playing in the mud. Some more dogs were playing tug of war, and a few of them were meditating, sitting in a corner.

My brother works at a doghouse? He should have told me. I could have given him tips on how to deal with the brats of our lot. He never tells me anything and never asks for help either. Well, it's his loss.

We entered and met the institute's head, possibly the principal of the doghouse.

"Hi, Oreo," I wagged my tail like a well-behaved student. "You will love it here."

Of course, I will, I thought. The place looks great, and it has so many toys! I replied with a bark.

"Let's give you both a tour."

What I liked best about the principal was that he was addressing us both, the parent and the student. He did not ignore me, as they do in most places. I didn't have to work for attention here, no extra wagging of the tail or twisting of the body. The tour lasted for about thirty minutes. The place housed ten separate dog rooms, if the dogs wanted to nap. The dogs were all unleashed and untied. We met at least five of the teachers playing with their wards. There was a tug of war, treat-distribution, hide-and-seek, fetch, and many more activities going on around the different parts of the premises. And it wasn't all just play; I saw dogs being trained on sitting, not barking, and not chewing shoes as well.

Thank God I am over that now, I thought, reminiscing when I was a puppy and had just shifted my house from the old family to my current one. For a few days, I was kept in the foyer where shoes and sandals were neatly stacked. I noticed that whenever the family members would go out, they'd wear those and leave me. In a fit of rage and revenge, I chewed six pairs of shoes and sandals the day they left me alone. Without sandals or shoes, how will they leave, right?

At first, they ignored me, but soon it became a game for me. If anyone wore sandals and started moving towards the door, I would catch the end and tug, tearing and shredding it. Sometimes it worked, sometimes it didn't. Other than one or two times, they ignored me. I kept chewing the sandals, and they kept buying new ones.

At one point, it stopped being fun anymore, and I stopped it altogether. Why give them a reason to buy a new pair of shoes and sandals? I wasn't getting new toys daily, was I? So why should they get to purchase new footwears so frequently? Yeah, I know, I am smarter than you think.

So, we rounded back to the main lobby after the tour, and Manish left me there. I assumed he would be at the property somewhere, perhaps as a teacher. However, he took his bag and went back into the same auto we'd come in. I was in a dilemma for the first time. Should I cry or should I enjoy this place? Feelings of being left alone took over, and I started howling. They ignored me. The principal who spoke kindly to me earlier did not come close or pet me. I kept on howling non-stop for twenty minutes. Then I noticed they had left me alone in my space. No dog or teacher paid attention to me. I looked at other dogs playing in the other sections of the house, and they all were enjoying themselves. They were offered treats, but I was not even asked.

The treats smelled really nice. Technically, I am not alone here. I have never seen that toy by the fence before. I should check it out. But what if Manish does not come back? He has to! He will! But what if he does not come back? I decided that I'll cross that bridge later. *Oh no, that dog is walking towards my toy!* I ran and grabbed the squeaky snake lying by the side of the fence before that dog could get near it. It was silky and squeaked when I pressed it. I started playing with it on my own, throwing it and jumping around with it.

"Oreo, are we getting settled now? Come on here, good boy, have this."

It was about time. They realised I needed treats too. Principal sir came and gave me an enormous slice of cheese. I started liking it there. I didn't notice how time flew by. The teachers assigned each dog a corner and instructed us to play only in our designated areas. We could mingle only when a teacher was present. I was fine with playing on my own and liked that better than trying to work around various issues associated with different dog personalities.

All the while, I kept an eye on the front area for vehicle activity. I missed Manish and wanted him to come and have fun with me as well. Every hour, I took a tour of the front yard to see for any signs of him. It was lunchtime, and he had not arrived yet.

"Oreo, lunch."

Typically, I would have waited for Manish, but the fragrance of chicken overpowered my senses, and I ran towards my food bowl. Chicken stew and rice, with actual pieces of chicken, not the packaged stuff. It was the best chicken I've ever had. With my tummy full, I drifted off to sleep.

At the resort, each dog had their own assigned area with a cushiony mat as their bed. It wasn't as comfy as my bed, but I'm not picky. They would assign you an area in open space with just small fences as boundaries between different dogs if you behaved. If not, it was a different story. I was busy with my siesta, when barks around me woke me up. I stretched in my bed and took in my surroundings. It was a bulldog who was chasing a much smaller breed of dog than him. What a coward. If you are in the mood to fight, at least choose an opponent of equal size. I follow this principle. I never bark or start a fight with dogs smaller than me. Even if they bark non-stop, I ignore them, thinking of them as spoiled children and move on. If I am in a fight, the opponent needs to be worthy.

The bulldog not only chased the smaller decorative dog, but also attacked and bit him hard. Principal and teachers came rushing in. One of them took the victim inside for treatment while the others grabbed the assailant and locked him in a room. The room's door had a see-through screen, enabling him to see what was happening outside, but he couldn't enjoy it. It was a timeout for him, after all.

As soon as the area emptied, I got up, stretched, and headed towards the room where he was locked. Out of curiosity, I peeked in from the door. The rogue bulldog lurched at me. He was not feeling even a bit of remorse. In order to irritate him, I started playing outside his door and, when he ignored me, I peed on his door. I got treats from the treats section and had them sitting in front of his door. I know I was gloating in my freedom, but it was my way of punishing him. I could see him growl and lunge at the door angrily. After an hour of teasing him and enjoying the spectacle, I finally left him to his grumbling—not out of pity, but because the game had lost its thrill. I returned to my bed, curling up and sinking into a peaceful nap. An hour later, I was roused by the commotion, as they finally let him out. Both the victim and the assailant were brought face to face, and I had to admit, it was impressive. They sat in front of each other, tension hanging thick in the air, but somehow, they managed to stay calm, thanks to the watchful eyes of the humans. They petted the bulldog and lavished him with treats, which only seemed to fuel his bravado. The bulldog, true to form, paraded the treats in front of me with a swagger that made me roll my eyes.

"Look at me," he seemed to say, flaunting his newfound goodies. Then, without a care, he settled down to relish them, clearly enjoying the attention. I couldn't help but feel a mix of annoyance and amusement. The drama had shifted, and while I had my fair share of fun, he was now basking in the glory of being the centre of attention. I smiled and appreciated his zeal; I could see a future friend in him.

I woke up around five, and that's when I started panicking. I could manage to be alone during the day, but once the sun goes down, I need my family. To add to my misery, other dogs started to leave for their homes, yapping and jumping with joy next to their family members. The bulldog's human mom was a sweet lady, and she patted him affectionately despite his destructive behaviour. Over-pampered, if you ask me. Not like me—well-groomed and well-behaved. Except for a few of the dogs, most left for their homes. I was really worried.

What happened to Manish? Where was he? And where was Prafulla? Are they fine? Is there any problem? They should have come for me by now. It's my walk time. My walker must be waiting for me. He'd think I wasn't punctual enough! What about my walk? Why are they not here? All the dogs are gone! Will I be spending the night here?

A wide smile spread across my face as I imagined the delicious chicken dinner. *No! Concentrate, Oreo,* I scolded myself. I prefer eating eggs at home. Please, God, send them to take me back home. God is quick to listen to my prayers. As soon as the words left my mouth, the auto I was looking for made its way to the front. Out came Manish, and I ran up to him. I waited at the front door by the principal's room for him to come and collect me.

"Oreo, *mera bacha,*" Manish petted me gleefully. "How are you?" He turned to the principal and asked, "Was he fine? Did he cry too much? He never enjoys being away from home. We tried to leave him at different facilities, but he never liked any place until today."

"No, he was definitely fine here. He took some time to adjust, but then once he settled, he became very playful. I must say, he is quite well-behaved."

"Thanks!" Manish was beaming as if the principal had praised him and not me.

"Did he eat well?"

"Yes, he licked his bowl clean."

Wow! So, you were watching me eat? No one likes to be monitored when they eat. These humans, I tell ya, they never understand, do they?

Ultimately, the boring conversation ended when they had analysed every minute of my day. So much for privacy. We boarded the auto and went back home.

The next morning, we followed the same routine; Manish dropped me off at the dog school and picked me up in the evening. It was a long drive and took us about an hour to reach there. From the third day onwards, a school van picked me up in the morning and dropped me in the evening. It was like going to a school, just like the kids I have seen. The only distinction was that I went without a backpack.

I loved going to school, except for that one time. I can manage anywhere during the daytime; don't roll your eyes, I certainly can. But at night, I long for the warmth of my family and the peace of my bed. I should have guessed it as things progressed, but my trust in my family fools me every time. That day, in the wee hours of the morning, I kept waiting for the van, but it did not come. Rishika was visiting, so I assumed maybe school was off in honour of her visit. Everyone was getting ready for the party. I was thrilled too. We were having a party in the house after a long time.

"Oreo, let's go."

Oh! Party in the open. I was in heaven. We sat, and our car zoomed past traffic, which was negligible. *Oh God, why are we at my school?* I wondered as we reached my dog school. I thought maybe the party was at my school, well, it would have to be a much better party than a human party. I was super excited. At the prospect, I jumped from the van even before it had stopped, eager to show Rishika and Priyansh around.

"He is so happy coming here," commented Priyansh.

"Yeah, thankfully!" said Rishika and I did not like her tone.

"The one is the only dog centre he approved, right?"

We went in, and I noticed there were more dogs than usual. *Well, the more the merrier*, I thought to myself. My family spent some time with me, and then they left. Well, I would have loved for them to be here, but it was fine. We had special treats that day. Lunch was a feast too. I had a good time, and now I was ready to go home. That day, most of the dogs stayed later than usual, and the principal and teachers got busy arranging beds inside the rooms. When they started moving mine inside, I started panicking. I wanted to go back home. I told him to wait for Manish. *He is coming*, I howled. I tried pulling the bed from the teacher's hand, but it was to no avail. I waited outside by the side of the fence till it was around nine, and the sound of crackers started hurting my ears. I went in hesitantly.

Dinner was served, and though I was in no mood to eat, the smell of freshly cooked fish changed my decision. The sound of crackers was increasing by the minute. It seemed like a lively party was taking place outside. Most of our caretakers had left by then.

"Happy New Year!" They had yelled at us before leaving us alone.

Suddenly, everything clicked into place: the sounds of crackers popping, the festive decorations strewn around the house, and the celebratory vibe. They had left me here alone, while they dashed off to enjoy the new year's party. *Selfish*, I thought, frustration rising within me.

What about my new year? Did anyone even think about how I wanted to celebrate the new year? I wondered in anger.

I resigned to my bed, dejected, thinking about ways I would want my new years to be. Just being close to my family and enjoying each other's company was in itself a celebration for me. I longed to snuggle with them, sharing in laughter and late-night snacks while watching TV like we used to with Mummy. Instead, I found myself alone, whimpering every time a loud cracker went off, numbing my ears.

Finally, after what felt like an eternity, the sounds began to fade around one o'clock, and the night returned to its quiet glory. The calm enveloped me like a warm blanket, and I could finally drift off to sleep. The next morning, my caretakers woke me up with gentle pats, and breakfast was a delightful treat—just what I needed to start the day.

Yet, as the morning wore on, I found myself in a familiar waiting game. It was around eight, and there was still no sign of my family. Just when I thought my heart couldn't take it anymore, I caught a glimpse of him.

Manish burst through the door and ran straight to me, wrapping his arms around me in a tight hug. In that moment, all my frustration and anger melted away. His warmth and enthusiasm filled the room, washing over me like a soothing balm. It was as if he had chased away the shadows of the night before, reminding me that no matter the ups and downs, the love we shared would always bring us back together. I nuzzled against him, feeling grateful for the joy of being reunited with my family.

“Happy New Year, Oreo!”

It was then that my new year started.

Life could have continued like this forever and ever, but then I wouldn't be telling you my story, right? As you can imagine, after a couple of months, destiny played its hand again and changed my world forever.

The coolness of the April evening enveloped me as I saw a car parked directly outside our home, with Manish packing it with my mattress and crate.

Oh God, not again!

My food was ready, and after I had my dinner, Manish and I got into the cab and started on a long road trip.

Chapter 24

We were on our way to Mumbai. I could smell the salty sea breeze as soon as we entered the outskirts of the city. But this time, before we reached Mumbai city, we made a stop. Yes, we stopped at various tea stalls throughout the night and for my late-night stroll, but this was a stop for documentation. We stopped at a government building, the same one we visited last time. We entered the building, and the security guard recognised me and Manish, asking about my well-being. He was a kind old man. Inside the building, I was checked and then given a certificate. I think it was an entry pass for Mumbai. But then I wondered, *how were they checking in the stray dogs? Who told them where they needed to go? Does this rule apply solely to dogs with human families?* I wanted to discuss this with the authorities, but time was short, and Manish was in a hurry.

"Oreo, *chalo. Jaldi,*" Manish said and pulled me in the car. After another thirty minutes on the road, we reached the same apartment. I think my family owns it. We spent a day and a half here before heading back to the airport. I was experiencing déjà vu. Everything was replaying itself: overnight travel to Mumbai, certificate at the government centre, same apartment stay, and then the long ride to the airport. It was an uncanny feeling, and I kept hoping it ended in the same way as it did the last time—with Manish and me returning to Ahmedabad together. I kept wondering about the logic behind it. *Was it necessary to travel such a long distance just to visit the airport and then return home?* We could have taken the same taxi home too, right?

Oh boy, little did I realise how wrong I was.

Using the same route, we reached inside the airport. I was inside the crate, with Manish's sweaty shirt giving me company. He certainly needed a lesson in privacy. We approached a counter, and a gracious lady talked to my brother. She came and talked to me as well, before taking my certificate and nodding.

Manish wiped his eyes more often this time, but everything else was the usual. He was behaving abnormally though. He would bend, look at me, and then move his face away. This became a cycle. I began feeling self-conscious. *Am I smelling that awful?* But they had bathed me only two days ago. I was busy contemplating Manish's strange behaviour when that lady came back again, this time smiling.

"All set?" She asked.

"Yes!" Manish bent down, this time he did not move his face away, and I could see tears rolling down his cheeks. He was crying, but why? He petted me from the narrow opening of the crate and said, "Take care, Oreo."

Before I could comprehend what was happening, my crate started moving. When the lady carrying me took a turn, I saw Manish standing at a distance, wiping his eyes. He was not coming. The realisation hit me like a brick. *I am being taken away from him. But why? Why are they doing this to us?* He kept crying, and I kept howling. *Why is my family being separated again? Who are these people? Why is this happening to me? What have I done wrong now?* I cried, howled, and whimpered with all my strength, but it was to no avail. I kept crying, and my crate kept moving. No one bent down anymore to look at me. The face I longed to see was no longer anywhere near me. I was taken to a cabin and left in the crate. Alone.

That was one of the worst days of my life till date. I was alone and scared, with no one in sight. The room had luggage everywhere, with enormous suitcases and bags neatly lined across the walls. The room had no windows, and someone had locked the door. I was feeling suffocated. I kept whimpering and praying. What would I have given to get my family back? Everything. *All my treats, every single one of my toys, and even my bed. Take everything, just get me back to my family. Please.* I kept praying and crying, crying and praying. But no one came, no one paid any heed to a crying dog, no one saw my tears, no one cared for my loneliness. This busy airport had everyone focused on their own things.

After what seemed like an eternity, a man showed up. He was short and petite. He opened my crate and leashed me. We left the room and went to the small park outside. It was pleasant to smell the fresh air, but I was seeking Manish. If I could only see him, I would run straight to him. We walked for about twenty minutes before coming back to the cabin. They served me Pedigree for dinner. No eggs. I don't eat Pedigree anymore; I only eat Blue Buffalo. They didn't even bother to check that. But I am not one to complain, and I was not hungry anyhow, so I pushed my bowl aside and just drank some water. Soon, it was time for me to return to my captivity in the crate. Only solace in that suffocating crate was the shirt my brother had left for me. He was not using the crate for his packing, I realised, he was giving me something to remember him by, something to comfort me. He knew. But how? If he knew, why didn't he prevent it from happening? If we hadn't come to this wretched airport, or this stupid city of broken dreams, nothing of this sort would have happened. With nothing else to occupy my mind, I pondered and tried to comprehend everything that could have prevented this from happening.

The door opened again, and this time, two men walked in along with the lady who'd started it all. At least she had the courtesy of talking to me.

"Do not worry, Oreo, everything will be fine. Happy journey!" And with that, I felt my crate move again. I was travelling again. I should have guessed. But I always travelled with my family. Why was I travelling alone this time? I snuggled my face inside Manish's shirt and cried. His smell was the only comfort I had. It gave me a sense of him being with me. We crossed room after room and were eventually out in the open.

I peeked outside my crate to look for my brother, but what I saw rendered me speechless. Planes were lined in a row, one after another. They were huge. I'd seen them in the sky before, but they always looked so small, like a bird. Up close, those giants were truly awe-inspiring. We halted near a plane, and my crate was lifted upwards. Air left my lungs. *Am I flying? But how? Did I die? Am I in heaven? How is my crate flying with me?* My crate was unloaded onto the plane's deck before I could make sense of anything. I was on the plane now. The place was filled with luggage. There was not a single person in sight. The plane's inside was a letdown compared to its exterior. From the outside, a plane was a beauty, a man-made marvel, but on the inside, it was plain and gloomy. There were no windows or lights, only luggage was kept all around the huge space. I wondered where people sat. There was no space. The people who'd come with me left me inside my locked crate. Before long, the door of the plane closed, and I was all alone with suitcases for company. The sound of the moving vehicles died, and it got really quiet.

Usually, I don't pity myself, but this time, man, I felt sorry for myself and my fate. Why me? I kept looking for answers. I alternated between whimpering, howling, and thinking, but not for long. I thought, *well, this is what it is. Get a hold of yourself. You are not one to pity yourself.* I was still alive, after all, which was great. My crate had some water, which was a blessing. But there was no place to pee. *Oh, that is why I have so many newspapers lining my crate. I get it now,* I thought. I had my bed and snake toy with me. I was on another adventure. I decided to see where the plane would take me. Worst case, I'd die. Nothing worse could happen, right? So, I relaxed.

Inside my crate, I stretched out and tried to sleep. Whenever fear of the unknown engulfed me, I reminded myself to think happy thoughts. I started playing the movie of my life in my mind. With each moment spent with my family washing over me, I felt a sense of peace settle in. But that calm was short-lived. Suddenly, a sharp jerk interrupted my reverie, and the entire plane began to shudder violently. My heart raced as the cabin rattled, and a wave of anxiety washed over me. The turbulence in the plane made it hard for me to calm down.

I guess I spoke too soon about death. I did not literally mean it, God. I want to see my family. I want to have chicken leg one last time. I started praying desperately. Right on time, a person entered the cabin. *Thank God for sending help! Thank you so much.*

I wagged my tail at the stranger, but he did not respond. I tried howling and telling him my plight, but he did not seem concerned. He just strapped my crate to two sides and left the cabin. *Why God? Why?* My resolve to be positive flew out the window of the windowless plane. *Why are you doing this?*

I had no idea why humans took pleasure in torturing inferior animals. I howled, whimpered, and then I lay down, resigning to my fate. The only thing I wanted to know was—what have I done to deserve it? Granted I was naughty, but I was not so dangerous to be left alone in a space as dark as hell with sounds as loud as thunder. I'd seen people commit murder on TV and get away with it. I haven't even killed a live chicken.

My misery was nowhere close to being over. A thrust pushed my crate forward, and the movement caused me to jump and hit the ceiling of the crate. I yelped in pain. The plane kept moving upwards. Maybe this was what flying was all about. I was no longer jealous of those birds in the sky. When I was a puppy, I always chased crows and sparrows from the terrace of my house. I ran after them. No matter what my speed was, I never caught them. They always flew high in the sky. They looked at me from up and always taunted me. A few of them even pooped on me. I wished for the power to fly so I could get back at them. I wished for many things: my autorickshaw, my beloved toy, and chicken for every meal. Why did God fulfil this wish of flying? Is it a chit-based selection where he grants whatever he picks? A lottery for your wishes? Lost in thought about the supreme, I didn't realise when the plane steadied. Feeling the wetness on my bed brought me back to my reality. In panic, I had wet the bed. I investigated the damage, pulled newspapers from the end of the crate, and put them on the wet space and made myself comfortable again. At that moment, I sensed complete stillness. Other than a loud whirring sound, there was nothing to signify that we were still moving.

But as they say, you get used to whatever is in your life. Whether good or bad. If it's consistent, it becomes a routine, and you get habituated to either pain or pleasure. I went to sleep in the same crate, where a while back I felt suffocated with the smell of my urine. When life gives you a lemon, you make lemonade, but what to do when that lemonade also spills? The sudden turbulence on the plane woke me. I jolted upright in my bed, ready to brace what was to follow.

The plane, which had been so silent till now, started shivering again. There was sharp shooting pain in my ears now.

Last time, I felt an upward movement of the plane, like we were going up. Now it was the complete reverse, like someone pulling us down. I felt alarmed. Are we falling? Did the engine brake? *I am going to die without my family being with me.* Such thoughts made me start whimpering, calling out to God.

The plane had increased its momentum and was now descending at a higher speed. Then, it touched the ground. I could perceive that because of the apparent jolt I got, and I could detect the shrieking voice of wheels touching the ground. Maybe God was not that cruel. The plane started cruising the ground. It initially travelled at a thousand kilometres an hour, then gradually slowed down before coming to a stop.

We landed and oh boy! I was glad. The ringing in my ears stopped, and the pressure vanished. The noise from the engine died. But I was alone and still paranoid. I continued my whimpers, this time with renewed energy. Someone might listen to me. *Hey, they listened once, they will listen again*, I thought. After around ten minutes of my non-stop howling, the door opened. A person walked in. I yelped in happiness. He removed the belts and took my crate out. I saw daylight, a revered sight I thought I'd never witness.

We reached a building, and once inside, they took me out of the crate. Never had I ever felt happier in my life. I savoured the sensation of freedom. They gave me water, which I gulped down quickly. I was starving too. Due to fear, my feeling of hunger had subsided in the plane, but when I felt safe, my stomach grumbled loudly. It was time for food. They fed me chicken stew, and I finished the whole can in record time—one minute. I was still missing my family, but hey, there was chicken. I couldn't let his death go to waste, right? On occasions such as this, social service was far more important, and seldom I'd foregone my oath to fast for my family. I finished one and a half cans.

With my stomach full and my feet on the ground, I came back to my senses. I wagged my tail in gratitude. My handler could not resist my charm any longer, and he petted me. I revelled in human touch. To my surprise, instead of putting me in the crate, they took me out for a stroll. In the evening, we ventured out into the open area next to my room. I felt the cool breeze and took in a long breath of fresh air, thanking God for small favours.

The place, as always, was crowded with people, but they were different. They appeared different from what I saw in Mumbai. They spoke differently and their manners were such too. As we are talking about the looks (although I don't care for race or ethnicity), I was amazed to see that some even had blue eyes. They all looked very fascinating to me. I was in a new place; one I had never been to. I observed my surroundings: no garbage in sight, and the roads were as clean as a house on the inside. I spotted a sign, and it read Paris. Oh, boy! I am in Paris, the epicentre of fashion!

Realising where I was, I quickly corrected my posture; I can't have a slouchy back here. I must uphold the name of my family. I walked as gentlemanly as possible. Seeing everyone dressed so well was exciting, even the dogs here were stylish. They were impeccably groomed with shiny collars and bows on their heads and necks; they truly embodied the fashion capital. I could feel how shabby I might look with overgrown nails, uncombed hair, and a boring silver-coloured metal collar. I wished I had worn something more proper. And on top of it, my leash was plain too. I tried to make up for what I was lacking in by keeping my posture proper and my gait correct. I held my head high and used my best feature to my advantage—my eyes. My pretty, expressive eyes did all the work.

People here were friendlier towards dogs. Everyone we met petted me and smiled. It was more to do with my looks than their nature, I believe. But reasons notwithstanding, I was a content canine. It was a pleasant walk filled with an abundance of love and appreciation, and after the emotional trauma I'd gone through, I believe I'd earned every bit of it.

We strolled for almost twenty minutes, and then the handler took a turn to return to my room. I didn't want to go. I yearned to uncover every nook and cranny of Paris. Just as we were about to turn back...

"Excuse me, for a sec," a pretty voice called from behind.

"*Si, senorita?*" the handler said.

"Is this your puppy?" I turned towards the sound, and she was a sight to behold. Such beautiful green eyes and warm smile. To top it all, she called me a puppy!

I wagged my tail in response.

"No, he just landed from India. I am just giving him a walk," the handler said, getting impatient.

"If you do not mind, I have a request," the lady said. "We will pay you for your time," she added before my handler could say no.

"For? And may I know your name please? I am John," he said. He was eager to talk now. "I cannot sell the dog though. He needs to take a flight again," he explained quickly.

"Aww too bad... I am Laura." The lady introduced herself as she bent down to pet me. "I would have kept you forever... You are just too adorable." She kissed me on my head. "But we actually need him for a shoot, you see. We are doing an ad for dog food, and our regular dog model got sick at the last minute. "I saw him from my car, and I cannot think there would be anyone more perfect than him," Laura explained, pointing towards me. "I can pay you as well as him for the time," she added.

"How much time would it take?" John enquired. "I need to drop him off before his flight takes off."

"We have the setup near the Eiffel Tower. We can be done in an hour."

"Let's do it!" John was more excited than I was, and I was pretty excited to be on TV.

As soon as John said yes, a car stopped in front of us. Calling it a car would be an understatement; it was the longest vehicle I'd ever seen. I jumped in immediately. It was gorgeous inside, with a sofa, fridge, and the softest dog bed!

"Nothing less than a limousine for my baby," Laura gushed as I got comfortable on the bed.

We set off on the beautiful Paris roads. I did not sleep in the van. While in Paris, I intended to see everything the city had to offer. I observed that the highways were more expansive and cleaner, and the traffic was non-existent. However, I did feel that the drivers here were lazy. For instance, our van kept on moving behind a car blindly. When the car stopped, our limo did as well, and when it moved, we did too. There were a couple of more lanes with columns of cars moving one after another. In between the lanes of cars, there was space for more cars to pass. Our driver, though, never tried to move past the other car. None of them did. I guess drivers here needed training in cutting lanes and overtaking other vehicles.

But when in Rome, do as the Romans do, so I avoided teaching him. I busied myself by checking out the streets of Paris. The slower the car moved, the more I could see. And then I saw it; I swear I stopped breathing for a moment. It was the famous Eiffel Tower! I could see it from the road, in its full glory. The lights on the Tower made it even more enchanting. The most stunning monument in the world was right in front of me. It was the only crowded place I'd seen so far. Massive lines of people were visible from the road. Our limo stopped, and we got out. I got out in style, at my finest behaviour, wagging my tail every thirty seconds. I did not want to come across as a wannabe or a snob—just someone who belonged to the world of glamour. Completely at ease.

The Eiffel Tower was right in the front. I looked up, and the setting sun was illuminating the monument. It was bathed in a golden glow. I was mesmerised.

"Let's get going. We need to get back to the airport as well," John said, pulling my leash.

I came back to reality. But to be honest, I wasn't very sure on what I should be doing?

I had thought it would be all about tasting food. Didn't they say it's for dog food commercials?

Instead, they first took me to a caravan. There was a groomer inside. He was standing with a brush and a hair dryer. I didn't like him. He looked exactly like my groomer back home. Are they going to give me a bath? I shuddered at the thought! Water and me, we never go along, you know it by now.

I pulled myself away. I wanted to jump out of the caravan.

"Hey, buddy? Come here," the groomer immediately said. His voice was friendly, so I relaxed.

Thankfully, it wasn't any bath. He combed my hair and blow-dried it a bit. Then, he tied the prettiest bandana on my neck. I was ready!

They took me to the grounds, which were decorated with so many bowls of food. But in the front, there was no one, only cameras! A lot of them!

A man far away was sitting with a small TV in front and a mic in his hand. He was surrounded by a lot of people. They were looking either at the TV or me.

I felt really special, like a king, you could say. And you know, it was quite easy.

The only catch was that I was not allowed to eat on my wish. I had to wait for the man to shout "action," and then one lady would take me near the bowl so I could eat as much as I wanted!

Next, one hour whizzed by. I never knew so many different flavours of food existed. And there is something called salmon and duck meat as well. I loved tasting everything, and they loved shooting me.

"Okay we need to leave now," John commanded.

"I will miss you, Oreo," Laura said a teary goodbye, and we were back again on the road. We reached the airport, and I was back on the flight again.

Chapter 25

Am I on a secret mission? Do I belong to a secret organisation that I am not aware of? Oh God! Did my family insert a diamond or something inside me and were smuggling it using me? They had taken me to the hospital, and the doctor was talking about a chip being inserted. *Was it a secret code being used for smuggling?* I paced inside my crate. I howled loudly. My future seemed uncertain to me.

The nightmare began all over again. The only thing that comforted me was the knowledge that we would eventually touch the ground again. I was not able to hear anything. This landing was worse, and I hit my head on the crate's ceiling harder than before. I had a terrible headache and earache, but I was thankful to be back on the ground... not sure where exactly though. I patiently waited for the cabin door to open, eager to see the daylight and breathe fresh air. I was tired of sitting in my pee. I wanted to take a bath for once. But to my horror, no one came. I started crying then. Still, no one came. I barked and barked. Finally, after an eternity, someone opened the door and moved my crate outside. It was a warm sunny day outside. And I was right; we landed after approximately ten hours of being airborne.

Hello! Take me out. Please! I am tired of being locked inside the crate.

But unlike Paris, no one paid attention to my cries here. I remained confined inside the box. They gave me water and dropped a few pellets of Pedigree inside my crate. I was not interested in eating or drinking; I wanted to get out. Instead of being taken outside for a walk, I was once again put into a van and taken to what seemed to be a warehouse. The place was packed with luggage, and workers were using huge cranes to move them from one place to another. I, too, was loaded and dropped by the crane at the other end of the warehouse. Out of one danger, on to another: my woes never ended. At least I was on the ground now. Counting blessings kept me alive, and I won't stop now. That, and my philosophy to keep trying, kept me going.

The warehouse was a dingy, neglected space. The air was heavy with an oppressive, musty odour, an unpleasant mix of rotting paper and damp, mouldy materials. The floor, uneven and stained, was scattered with debris.

In one corner, a pile of discarded boxes and broken pallets formed a haphazard mound, their contents now a breeding ground for insects. The room felt vast and empty, devoid of any sign of life or movement, amplifying the eerie silence that surrounded me. It was reeking of spilt oil and fungus.

It had been over fifteen hours since I last had anything to eat or drink, and the ache in my stomach was growing unbearable. My throat was completely parched from the lack of water, and it made me feel more and more desperate. Yet, as I looked around, it was clear that the staff didn't notice my suffering. They moved about their tasks with indifference, seemingly oblivious to my plight.

Sometimes, someone would come by to pet me, but it felt like fleeting kindness in my growing agony. No one thought to feed me or take me out for even five minutes. I wagged my tail eagerly at everyone who walked past my room and at every crane that came to pick up supplies, but they all seemed to ignore me, as if I were just another piece of luggage left behind.

It was a painful realisation that I was nothing more than luggage. The thought of dying alone in this dark, forgotten space filled me with sorrow. What I wouldn't give for one last walk in the open air, to savour my favourite chicken meal one more time.

As another hour ticked by, the weight of my situation dawned on me. I sank deeper into my crate, a mix of resignation and longing swirling in my heart. I tried to accept my fate, but the flicker of hope still lingered, whispering that maybe, just *maybe*, someone would remember me and change my story before it was too late.

The crane, with its steady, rhythmic movement, was an omnipresent entity in this dark world. I had grown accustomed to its mechanical grunts and groans, the shuddering vibrations reverberating through the floor as it lifted and lowered boxes. But what I wasn't prepared for was the moment it picked up my crate.

The sudden jolt as the crane's hook latched onto my crate jolted me from my resigned state. Panic, anxiety, and confusion gripped me. As the crate lifted off the ground, I whimpered softly, unsure of where I was being taken or what awaited me beyond the confines of the cold, forgotten warehouse.

Where am I going to be dropped now?

As my crate was lifted and moved, I caught a glimpse of light emerging ahead through a narrow alley. At first, the light was faint, but as the crane continued its course, it grew more intense and blinding.

Is this the tunnel to heaven? I thought, feeling a wave of uncertainty washing over me. I braced myself for the unknown, my heart pounding in anticipation.

When the blinding light finally began to fade, I opened my eyes, and to my surprise, I found myself confronted with the familiar, comforting faces of Nikhil, Lipika, and Papa. I was confused.

I could understand seeing Nikhil and Papa during what I feared might be the end of my journey, but Lipika? *Why was she here?*

I was busy thinking about this unexpected reunion, trying to make sense of it all, when it hit me—*perhaps this wasn't the end.*

As the light began to soften, you could see more clearly that Nikhil, Lipika, and Papa were standing on the ground, their faces lit with excitement and happiness. I was still suspended high in the air; my crate being held aloft by the crane. The sight below made me question my reality. Was this an illusion? Or perhaps a sign that I was indeed still alive.

Does it mean my ordeal is over? I kept looking at them, lest I lose them again. The descent of the crate felt like a gentle return to reality, where the familiar faces of my loved ones were no longer distant or unreachable. They did not abandon me. As I approached the ground, I could see them more clearly, their joy evident in their eyes. Oh man! I cannot express what I felt: anger, happiness, relief. Everything rolled into one emotion.

While I was busy organising my thoughts, Lipika pushed her hand inside my crate, and I licked it.

"Oreo, finally you are here!" she shouted with joy.

Although I somewhere felt she had something to do with my travelling, I chose not to show any anger. She was, after all, family, and I was hungry for human attention. *I will take my revenge later. Now it's a family reunion*. I thought. They exchanged papers and took my crate outside the warehouse.

As the crate door swung open, I bolted out, finally escaping the confines of the crate. The warm sensation of bright daylight, and the fresh air made me feel more alive.

As I looked around, taking in the new surroundings, I realised I was free. I was reunited with my loved ones, and that was satisfying. The freedom to move and explore once again and to bask in the sun and be able to mark my territory cannot be expressed in words.

I was free from the crate but was still processing the intense emotions and experiences I had just endured. After all that, I was still alive. When I realised the magnitude of what I had gone through, a shiver ran through me, and I started trembling. My family sensed my discomfort and surrounded me. They petted me, hugged me and brought me food and water. Everything was comforting, but the panic I was feeling did not subside.

"Let's take him home. He will feel better there."

Miss know-it-all spoke and as usual, everyone agreed. They brought back my crate again and asked me to go inside. I did not budge. I was no longer a beggar. I put down my foot—I was not getting inside that crate. Who knew where it would take me?

"He doesn't want to go in the crate."

"It's understandable, he is afraid of the crate now."

Finally, the crate had to travel alone in the trunk of the car, because I sat in the backseat with Lipika. Papa and Nikhil sat in front. *Finally, I was free from that crate. What a relief!* I was filled with overwhelming joy, my heart brimming with happiness. We started our ride. I was unsure where I was. The roads were wider and cleaner, and everyone seemed to follow the traffic rules. *Am I in Paris again?* But it felt different. Paris was colder and more magnificent. I kept looking for signs and boards as we crossed the airport again. I averted my gaze upon spotting a plane. I no longer wanted to fly. As we passed the airport, I saw the sign: San Francisco Airport. I was in the United States of America!

I could not believe it! They made me travel across the seven oceans without even asking me. What if I had not wanted to come to America? They might have had an interest in coming here, as this was the land where dreams turned into reality, but I was quite content in Ahmedabad. They never gave me a choice. I stopped myself from thinking too much. At least I was with my family, well, half of them anyway, and that was all that mattered. To divert my mind, I started observing the surroundings as we drove. No cows or donkeys could be seen on the road, and no dogs crossed the roads. There were no herds of goats walking in the middle of the road. It was even devoid of people. It felt like a ghost town, only cars and nothing else. *Maybe this is what I would see if I time-travelled to the future, scarcity of people and abundance of technology,* I thought. I like people and enjoy watching other creatures of God way more than technology. This was unnerving for me. I was used to riding autos in India, where we passed not only people but cows, dogs and goats on the road. Everyone shared it. I felt homesick. The never-ending ride continued. Exhausted, I settled in the back seat as Lipika gently stroked me to sleep. She was probably feeling guilty and was trying to win back my favour. Fat chance.

"Oreo, get up. *Ghar aa gaya*."

Chapter 26

The house was massive: a big hall and too many rooms. Each room was more grandiose than the last. Despite its beauty, I could not appreciate it. The trauma of my recent experience loomed over me, and I was driven by a singular fear.

I ran from end to end.

I took respite only after checking every nook and corner. As I entered again from the garage, I found myself in the family room, a cosy space with plush sofas and a large television. Next to that was the kitchen and dining hall, where the aroma of freshly baked bread still lingered in the air. The formal living room was directly ahead. To the left of the living room were the three bedrooms. They faced each other in the gallery. I darted into every room, flinging open doors, peering under beds, and behind curtains. The house was totally fine; there were no whirring sounds, no hidden engines, and no cabins with metal doors. My heart pounded in my chest as I searched for any sign of wheels. I had to be sure, absolutely certain, that this place was on the ground. The mere thought of flying again, of being lifted off the earth and thrown into the sky, filled me with dread.

I listened carefully, but all I could hear was the gentle hum of the air conditioning and the distant chirping of birds outside. The fear that had driven me to this exhaustive search began to dissipate.

I was safe.

But there was no water either. I retraced my steps, starting from the garage and moving through the family room, the kitchen, and the dining hall. I scanned the countertops and peeked under the table, but my bowls were nowhere to be seen. Even the bathroom sinks were dry, and the bathtubs empty. I was thirsty. My family was in their own world, running after me. Even Papa.

"Calm down, Oreo. You are home now."

Yeah, I will calm down if you give me water. No one paid heed, as usual, I had to improvise. I remembered seeing a bathroom at the end of the gallery during my first inspection of the house, so I ran towards it. My paws padded quickly along the hallway, the urgency of my thirst driving me forward. The toilet bowl had water in it. Without hesitation, I approached and drank to my heart's content.

"*Chee*, Oreo! It's dirty water!" Lipika was behind me.

Maybe if you all paid a little more attention to me, I wouldn't have had to resort to drinking toilet water, I barked.

Hopefully, now she'd understand what I needed. I was thirsty, and my family was not attentive to my needs. What could I do? But that water was not enough, and I was still parched.

Oh, wait a minute! I sprinted straight to the prayer room and, as expected, I found a bowl of holy water kept there. Papa always said holy water is always good.

He would offer me holy water during my illness back in Ahmedabad, and I got better after drinking it. As I went for the water, the *diya* fell down.

"Oreo!" Papa came running into the room.

"Move away from the *pooja* room," he commanded, picking up the *diya*.

"Oh, sorry, Oreo. He is thirsty. We forgot to give him water," Lipika said and sprinted to the kitchen.

It is time you realise, geniuses. Now they got moving. There was a fresh water and food dish placed in the living space.

"He is not behaving normally," Nikhil remarked. "Why is he pacing up and down so much?"

"He is agitated," Lipika started with her psychology lecture.

"Wait, Mummy is calling," she said.

Thank God for small mercies.

"Yes, Mummy. Oreo is fine," Lipika explained.

Someone please ask her what *she* will do after stepping out of the horror ride? How could I relax? What did they know about being locked up in a crate? And now she is telling Mummy that I am fine.

"Oreo, how are you, *beta*?" I heard Mummy's voice and immediately my ears perked up.

I am not feeling well. I am missing you a lot. It's been long, I howled.

"I will come to meet you soon, Oreo. I will get permission from the doctor in some time," Mummy replied (as always, she understood me).

"You go for a walk and then sleep, okay?" she concluded and disconnected the phone.

"I will take him for a walk. It will calm him. Oreo, *chalo*," Nikhil said and opened the garage door.

I was more than ready to go. Once outside, I realised that so far, it was the most relaxing part of my day. I relished the open sky. There were neither any sounds of the rumbling engines nor any cages to hold me. We went to a nearby park, which was filled with lush green trees. The soft breeze on my face further made me believe I was free. I would have kept on walking and walking, but my brain was tired, and I was exhausted. I pulled on my leash towards the direction of our home. Nikhil understood, so we walked back home.

When we returned home, boiled eggs were waiting for me. Nikhil fed me with his hands, yes, not with a spoon but his hands. After eating, I wanted to lay down and sleep, but where was my bed? I remembered it was spoiled in the journey because of all the times I had to pee on it. Unable to keep my eyes open, I slumped on the wooden floor and drifted off into oblivion amongst the chatter of my sleeping arrangement.

"The bed is unusable."

"We need to get a new one immediately."

I heard the car start. *Was I left alone again?* I got up, alarmed. *Not again!* They could not leave me alone, not today of all days. How heartless! I started howling loudly.

"*Ohm... Ohm... Ohm...*" I heard Papa's voice. He was talking to me.

During his *pooja*, he called me *Ohm*. I ran up to him in the *pooja* room. He looked at me and smiled. I slept by his side as he finished his *pooja*.

The sound of the garage door opening disturbed my sleep.

"Oreo, come here. See what we got for you."

A new bed and blanket were lying near the living room couch. Seconds later, I comfortably went back to sleep in my new bed.

I have a blurred memory of the next few days. Most of my time was spent sleeping. I do not know why, but I suddenly wanted to sleep all day and wake up at strange times. Apart from sleeping, I explored the huge backyard of my new house. That was a surprise. It was the first house where I saw such a huge open space. I spent a lot of time outside, sleeping under the tree. This place was calmer, and apart from occasional cars passing by, that also without honking, it was very quiet here. There were no hawkers selling their stuff, and I did not hear any dogs barking or howling. The lack of horns blaring came as a surprise to me. It was eerie to observe cars passing by without honking. Maybe cars in this area weren't advanced and didn't have that feature yet. Whatever it was, I disliked too much silence. I was not used to it. But it didn't matter whether I liked it or not, I had to get used to it, and with time, I did.

Another thing that unsettled me was the absence of garbage in our area. It unnerved me to not even find a single polythene cover on the road. I mean, it was impossible that these people discarded nothing. I had seen garbage being put in bins at my home, and if nothing else, I was sure my eggshells had to be thrown somewhere. This disturbed me to no end, and I took it upon myself to investigate and get to the bottom of it.

In the morning and evening, during my walks, I kept my nose open to observe any change in the area's smell. I continued looking for something different. I kept at it for an entire week, and eventually, my hard work paid off, as it always does.

On Tuesday morning, there was something different outside every house, including mine. There were some huge cans kept out, and I could smell them from far; they were what I had been hunting for. It was the smelly, decayed leftovers. The fragrance of chicken wafted through the cans along with the leftover fish. I was in garbage heaven. But to my dismay, all of them were closed shut, and I could only smell from afar. At least I had solved the mystery.

On my way back from my walk, I spotted a gigantic truck. It had a crane attached to its side. At once, I hid behind Nikhil. I was not prepared to be picked by a crane again. The truck slowly approached our street. I started sweating. The truck stopped alarmingly close. I took a few steps back while Nikhil was oblivious to my plight. Its claws started moving in our direction. I tugged at my leash and moved further away from the crane. To my surprise, the claws, instead of taking me up, picked up the huge trash cans and emptied them into the truck. *Oh, thank God!* I came out from behind Nikhil. I was not afraid anymore. I understood now: garbage was not safe here. Truck monsters were after them. That explained why there was no garbage to be found on the street.

I made a mental note to go for a stroll super early on Tuesdays. That day was my only chance to perceive the aroma of each house before the monster truck took the garbage away.

This country was indeed different. I never had to work so much for garbage. And even after this, all I could do was sniff as I couldn't go near the garbage cans.

My walks to the park might have been good exercise, but they certainly lacked excitement. The well-maintained pathway, although clean and orderly, offered little in terms of interesting scents or intriguing discoveries. Without any trash cans to inspect or stray droppings to investigate, the experience was quite monotonous.

I excelled at sniffing, a skill I am proud of. I could detect even the faintest trace of a scent and would dig until I found its source. Most often, it was an insect or some rotten fruit lying buried, but occasionally, I found more exciting stuff, like a chicken bone or a fish tail.

My walks followed the same route each time: a straight line to the park and back. Along the way, I saw numerous side streets branching off from the main road, each one holding the promise of new adventures and hidden treasures.

If only I could make them understand that walking isn't just about moving from one place to another. Even zombies could manage that. For us living beings, a walk is an opportunity to sniff, smell, explore, dig, and mark our surroundings. Only then can it truly be called a walk.

I strategised. I analysed and determined who among Lipika, Nikhil, or Papa would be more flexible. Papa wasn't a big fan of the whole poop-scooping routine, so he wasn't as reliable for walks. Nikhil, being headstrong, proved difficult to sway.

But Lipika, she was different. I noticed that if I played my cards right and did things that made her happy, she'd be more willing to let me lead the way. She was more emotional and easily influenced by my antics. So, I chose to stick with her for my adventures, knowing she'd be more likely to give me the freedom to explore the routes I desired.

This is how the scene would unfold. When we reached the house that usually didn't make the cut for their walks, I would start by pretending to be disinterested, almost like I was resigned to the idea of sticking to the usual path. But as soon as Lipika's tone softened with compliments and affection, with a deft nudge and a gentle pull, I guided her towards the lane I had in mind. It was a bit of a game—a dance of wills between me and her.

"Oreo! Which street did you bring me to! I have not seen such a beautiful collection of flowers anywhere nearby."

I pulled her towards a small heap of sand, and I was right. I dug out a small piece of leftover chicken thigh. Ecstasy!

"See? This is beneficial for both of us!" I told her with the bone in my mouth.

Life was gradually returning to a sense of normalcy. I was growing comfortable in the new house, adjusting to the big backyard and the constant chatter of Lipika. The house was still a work in progress, with renovations keeping everyone busy. From morning until evening, the trio was engaged in their respective tasks: Lipika busied herself with painting various parts of the house, her creative touches slowly transforming the space. Nikhil spent his time aligning things with his tools. Papa, with his passion for the outdoors, dedicated his efforts to the backyard, nurturing the garden and making the most of the open space.

Papa was always the busiest of them all, and his passion for his work in the backyard was evident. I admired his dedication and wanted to be part of it, especially since his tasks resonated with me. He had a knack for digging, a skill I shared and loved. Every morning, he would head to the backyard, where he meticulously marked out mud lanes before digging between them.

I watched intently from the side, fascinated by his work and eager to be part of it. One day, however, I noticed something odd. As Papa dug, he began dropping items from his pockets into the holes he had carefully excavated. It seemed like he was growing tired and perhaps losing track of his actions. To my dismay, he would then cover up the holes he had worked so hard to dig, only to start the process over again.

My heart ached for him. He was stuck in a cycle of digging, covering, and dropping items that appeared like seeds, seemingly unaware of the repetitive nature of his tasks. I wanted to help, but when I approached him to assist, he chased me away, not realising the trouble he was in. So, I decided to wait patiently for him to go inside the house.

Once he was out of sight, I took it upon myself to dig up the holes he had inadvertently covered. I also searched for the items he had dropped, discovering peanuts and black grams buried within. Carefully, I picked them up in my mouth and carried them back to him, hoping he would appreciate the effort and reward me for my help.

Can you point out my error in the above scenario? I'm still puzzled by the intense scolding I received that day. Even helping has its consequences, I realised that day. I think my old man was hitting that dreaded sixty-year mark. Instead of treats, I got a scolding.

Scolding or no scolding, I loved being with my old man. He scolded me if I entered his *pooja* room. He berated me if I helped him in the garden, and he reprimanded me if I did not eat my food. But he conversed with me the longest too.

"Oreo, I am heading to the temple. Will be back in thirty minutes."

"Oreo, I will drop these mails to the post office." Before he went anywhere, he informed me so that I wouldn't be worried.

I was accustomed to Papa's presence, a comforting constant in my life here in the USA. Everything felt right with him around. So, when he started packing suitcases, it immediately set off a wave of anxiety and confusion. I darted around, hoping to understand what was happening, trying to piece together why this was happening again.

When he finally approached me, it was with a gentle touch and a reassuring voice. "Oreo, I am journeying to India," he said, his hand soothing my fur. "Eat your food on time, okay?" His words were meant to comfort, but they only highlighted the fact that he was leaving. I wondered why it wasn't Lipika leaving. Why was he not taking me with him?

As they loaded the suitcases into the car and drove away, I chased after them, but the garage door closed abruptly in my face. The world outside seemed so far away, and I felt a pang of sadness and confusion. Now it was just the three of us in the house. Life changed again.

Chapter 27

Having been in the US for a while, I've observed something peculiar: every dog I see is on a leash. I am not sure what their laws are at the country level, but I haven't yet seen any unleashed dogs. In India, dogs roamed around freely on the streets, ate garbage and drank sweet muddy rainwater from puddles, all without a leash. In my opinion, they were better off than the dogs in America. I know I am the unfortunate one, i.e., a leashed dog. In India, at least I could derive pleasure from seeing the free ones, walking liberally. It was a feeling you might have upon seeing your siblings prosper. So, I aspired to be a catalyst for transformation, symbolising resistance and revolution. The 'chain culture' represents a stifling environment that I felt compelled to break free from.

It pained me to see everyone chained here. There were times when I considered starting a rebellion, and even now I am trying to. I have already run leash-free on the streets of the USA. It's easier to escape from this house as it's on the corner of the street. On top of it, there is no fence; it's just a matter of someone leaving the door ajar or some kid pressing the garage button.

So, I tried running in all the streets around my house, to seek dogs, talk to them, and encourage them to speak up. But I could only do it if I saw someone walking without their owner or on a leash. And that is yet to happen. I am running out of time because my family is putting up fences around our house. They took such a drastic decision because of that stupid car. If you are wondering which stupid car, then let me tell you a not-so-old incident from my wanderings.

It happened when a four-year-old opened the garage door for me. He was in the garage one morning and he asked me, "Oreo, do you want to go out?" *What a sweet little boy*, I thought.

I moved closer to the garage door in response. He grabbed the remote, opened the door, and I sprinted outside like lightning.

Within a minute, I could see Nikhil, Lipika, and the kid's father running after me. I ran faster as they were catching up with me. I ran towards the street to get away. Right then, a car zoomed past me. Just two inches away from me. I froze. If I would have been a step further on the street, I would have died.

"Oreo! Are you alright?" Everyone came running to me. Nikhil ran his hand over my body to check if there was any blood.

I am fine, I tried telling them.

"We will have to get the fence," Nikhil muttered, checking the perimeter of the house.

My human family gets scared very easily. They say I escaped once, so I could escape again. After that, too, I ran outside many times. I am a brave dog. Once, I made

Lipika run behind me for an hour before I let her leash me. I had told you guys that I would take my revenge, didn't I? One day, I did just that. She was alone at home with me, and there came a deliveryman at the door. She opened the door for the Amazon package, and I slipped out through the crack.

"Oreo, stop!" She ran after me. Realising she'd forgotten something, she ran back to the house, locked it and ran behind me again. That gave me time to increase the distance between us.

"Oreo... Oreo..." I could hear her voice, but I chose not to come into her view. I couldn't care less. It certainly was fun. It had been more than an hour, and she was still running behind me. She was sweating, completely tired, and was almost on the verge of crying. She ran street after street behind me. I took pity on her and came into her field of vision. Yeah, she could have never caught me without my help. I am also wonderful that way.

The kids have helped me escape more than a few times. Ishaan was the one who made me realise that kids could be friends too, rather than the nuisance I thought they were.

"Oreo! Oreo! Oreo's the world's best dog." I heard the chant before I saw him.

"Oreo, my boy, I love you!" he declared, petting me eagerly.

He entered the house chanting that, even before he saw me. Till the time he was at the house, he was just by my side. If I urinated outside, he would join me. If I ventured to chase the cat away, he barked alongside me. Yes, he barked with me. If I made my way to drink water from my bowl, I had to navigate through his hands to reach my water bowl.

He kept up a constant chant of 'Oreo'. Now when I think of it, I guess it's possible that he viewed me as a divine being. What kind of worship is that exactly, I have no idea. I was used to fanfare; I have been famous. However, even I couldn't handle this excessive amount of randomness. That day when he left, I thanked God. Hours after he left, his voice continued to echo in my ears. I felt a sense of compassion for God that day, considering the multitude of people who incessantly chant their name day and night. How do they manage to preserve their hearing? As if this was not enough, he even wrote a poem for me. Anyway, for now, let's get back to how he, with utter sweetness, assisted my escape!

He helped me get out of the house countless times. My daring escapades and knack for creating chaos have inspired some of the most thrilling scenes on screen.

Like that time when we were in the backyard: I was engaged in a repetitive back-and-forth movement near the exit door, when he questioned whether I wished to go outside. My restless pacing must have been a clear signal of my desire for freedom. Naturally, I showed my excitement by wagging my tail and increasing my pacing. He unlocked the door for me, and I wasted no time in darting off without any restraint. Just outside the house was the main road, so I ran.

I was running alongside the road, with Nikhil running close behind me. I might have kept running had I not looked to my right. I saw a lake filled with ducks. Without a second thought, I neither looked right nor left and just crossed the street.

While crossing, I heard a loud crash. I looked back and saw a car braking hard, leading to a pileup on the road. Though I felt a brief urge to stop and ask if they needed any help, I knew I couldn't literally do that. Instead, I briefly paused to ensure there was no major damage. Both the drivers were coming out, probably to chat with each other. I could have stopped to hear their conversation, but driven by the allure of the lake, the smell of ducks, and the promise of fish, I resumed my run towards the water.

I reached the lake; it was worth the run and much more! Ducks were gliding across the water, their ripples the only disturbance to the otherwise calm surface. In my opinion, ducks are like chickens' NRI cousins, who can even swim! I cannot fathom any other difference.

I glanced back just to make sure Nikhil is fine. He was coming towards the lake, sweat on his face. Our eyes locked, and I could see relief in them. Either he was glad to see me, or just thankful to be able to get away from those drivers: I am not very sure.

Before I go on exploring further, let's have a heart-to-heart. A little *gyaan* from me to you. Don't worry, I will not bore you with a lengthy self-help talk. Just a few words of wisdom, which we dogs have a lot of! Trust me on this. First of all, thank you for being my companion through these chapters of my life. And truly, what a journey it has been so far! From the streets of Bangalore to the Taj Mahal, and the iconic Eiffel Tower: I have seen it all. Do I consider myself lucky? Well, I am not too sure. Would I have preferred a calm life with my whole family in Bangalore? You bet I would!

But I am equally thankful for the experiences I have had: good, bad, and the ugly. The fear I have felt, the feeling of loneliness and helplessness, I'm grateful for it all. The journey shaped me into who I am today. If you ask me what I feel now, it would be peace and complete acceptance of the life I have. I feel surrounded by love, and my family is here with me. I am content, but not tired. So, adventures will continue. Life is nothing but a sum total of our adventures, and my autobiography is bound to be a million pages, for sure!

What I would suggest is this: live life to the fullest and accept every situation wholeheartedly, even if it's totally devastating or unfair. Accept that it is what it is, and from there, try to change what you can and look for doors. I guarantee you; doors will always be there if we just look!

Now, I believe I've trained you too. My family may be stubborn as ever, but you'll do as I say, right?

Oh, Nikhil's coming... until next time then, folks!

"Oreo, that's it for today! *Ghar chalo*."

